ORDEAL

John Prescott

CENTER POINT LARGE PRINT
THORNDIKE, MAINE

This Center Point Large Print edition
is published in the year 2014 by arrangement with
Golden West Literary Agency.

The text of this Large Print edition is unabridged.
In other aspects, this book may vary
from the original edition.
Printed in the United States of America
on permanent paper.
Set in 16-point Times New Roman type.

ISBN: 978-1-62899-252-6

Library of Congress Cataloging-in-Publication Data

Prescott, John, 1919–
Ordeal / John Prescott. — Center Point Large Print edition.
pages ; cm
Summary: "Six strangers are set afoot in the desert when their stage
bound for San Diego overturns while escaping an Indian attack"
  —Provided by publisher.
ISBN 978-1-62899-252-6 (hardcover : alk. paper)
ISBN 978-1-62899-321-9 (pbk. : alk. paper)
1. Large type books. I. Title.
PS3531.R434O73 2014
813'.54—dc23
                                                    2014025807

For Kitty Lou and Bill Mitchell, fine people

ORDEAL

1.

All morning the coach clattered and banged along the stony road, throwing a storm of gravel at its underside and raising a plume of dust that stained the air behind it.

But now as noon came on, it started slowing; gradually the roadbed changed and the ragged jolting grew less. When the coach drew nearer to the foot of the long grade that climbed up into the pass of barren red stone that lay ahead, it moved still slower, until finally it settled upon itself and came to a halt. Through the window by his seat, Muller could hear the wheels leave off their heavy grinding. The horses gathered their hoofs beneath them and the noisy trace chains quit rattling. Save the jiggling of the body in the leather thorough braces, like an animal breathing after heavy labors, there was sudden quiet about them. With headway lost, there came a boil of dust that seeped up through the cracks and hung suspended in the desert sunlight streaming through the upper part of the windows on the side where Muller sat. But as the road went off to the northwest on this leg of the journey, the sun was at a height and angle that kept the worst of it from coming directly down onto him.

Even so, he felt the pressing closeness of the

heat as the circulation of air died. And, like the others, he stirred and humped around in his seat in order to get more comfortable. Then, as they began to hear the driver working at the hatch above their heads, they grew more quiet.

From his corner, Muller saw the iron hasp wiggling as the driver fiddled with it. The hatch lay in the forward wall, and just above the head of a girl who sat across the aisle from Muller. Her name was Hale—Miss Maggie Hale, as he had heard her give it to the division superintendent in Tucson when she'd got on in the early morning. She was good to look at, too, as pretty as you'd ever want, and had a way of holding her head that made him think of Helen, who was waiting for him in San Diego; at least he hoped that she was still waiting for him. Having her in his mind's eye, he saw that she would be about the same in age and size as Miss Hale; and there looked to be a likeness in their color, too, which ran to fair skin with dark hair and eyebrows.

Still, on making as close a study of her as he dared to make without her noticing, he saw differences between them, too. Likely, did he know her, he'd find plenty, but what drew his eye the quickest was the clothing she wore. Her dress was of a cut and slickness passing anything he'd ever seen on Helen, and seemed to indicate she'd done some living in the world. Of course, he could be wrong about her. But once, on seeing her face in an unguarded moment, it seemed so grave and knowing that he couldn't doubt she'd seen things that Helen could only imagine.

Miss Hale was sitting in the middle of the seat, with a man on each side of her. The one who sat across from Muller was an old man named Otto Wagner. He would easily be the oldest in the coach, a man who had a head of white hair and a beard which, saving the little streaks of yellow from tobacco juice, was white, too. Judging by his age, he could be Muller's grandpa; but his eyes were young and snappish, and he kept them busy scanning the country.

Wagner was a talker, too, and liked to tell of glory holes and chimneys that he'd known of in the mining days before the war had broken out. To hear him, you would think he was a man who'd struck it rich, until you saw his shabby camp clothes.

On the other side of Miss Hale sat a younger man. His name was Ansel Jager, and he was perhaps thirty or forty years younger than Wagner. Jager seemed nearer Muller's age, maybe beyond a little, but he was a bigger man than Muller was. Since he didn't dress in any special way, you couldn't tell much from that; but as he hadn't much to say, he seemed the sort who'd rather be left alone.

He was one to make you wonder, though. Wagner had been on the coach when Muller had got on at Mesilla Valley on the Rio Grande, back a number of days; but Jager was another Tucson passenger, who'd gotten on with Miss Hale. While at first they didn't seem to know each other, it wasn't long before Miss Hale was leaning over to talk to him off and on. What made you wonder was his way of paying no attention to what she said. All the while she talked, he only brooded out the window and looked annoyed and sullen.

By the window in the other corner, back on Muller's side, sat Lieutenant James V. Patterson, and he had been at pains to let them know that. Along with Wagner, he'd been riding from St. Louis, where the line split for its run to the West Coast. Long ago he'd learned the shady side on which to sit, and he made a habit of leaving his map case on his seat whenever a stop was made. That way he'd have it saved for him when they got started again.

Not that Muller especially cared. Sitting where he was, he didn't have to look at Patterson very often; nor could Patterson see him, unless he stretched his neck and looked around the man between them. But he only did that once, when Muller had got on, and after that ignored him as maybe being of little account.

The name of the man between them was Alfred Huston, and from Muller's view of him he was the only man aboard who looked a gentleman. When Huston had got aboard at Fort Bowie back there in Apache Pass beneath the Chiricahuas, Muller'd thought he might be with the government—maybe a commissioner, or even an Indian agent. But when he saw the derringer sticking out of Huston's waistcoat pocket, he wondered if he was a gambling man. There was always plenty of them hanging around the Army posts and garrisons, waiting to take your money. God knew there'd been plenty of them at Craig. He was clean, too, and smoothly dressed, the way they liked to look, but he was quiet, a gentle quiet, and you couldn't really do more than guess.

It didn't help to know where he was going, either. All of them, according to the waybill, were going to the Coast but old Wagner. As he'd told them maybe a dozen times, he meant to leave them when he reached Yuma. From there he'd take a paddle-wheeler up the Colorado to Ehrenburg or La Paz, where he planned to work the placers in the gold fields newly found up that way.

The very thought of Yuma in July, in this scalding heat, gave Muller pause to wonder at the kind of man who would get off at such a place, even to dig for gold.

Just then, however, the hatch opened, and he saw the driver looking down at them. His face was like a picture set in a frame, the gray mustachios sloping from his long nose, the weather-rusted cheeks, and the hat brim putting his eyes in dark shade.

He was smiling, and the sunlight lay upon his jawbone and his big yellow teeth.

"Are we makin' it?" he said. "Comfy, are we?"

Nobody said if they were comfy, or if they were making it. Asking such was just the brand of humor the drivers used with passengers.

He didn't seem to expect an answer, anyway. When no one spoke, he only gave his nose a pull and kept smiling.

"Well, that's fine," he said then. "I'm glad to hear it. Surely wouldn't want no one unhappy. Tell you what, I thought to mention there's a pass coming, and that pretty soon now, I'm going to ram it. Be best if all of you should get a grip on something, so's to stay put."

"I guess we ought to thank him," Wagner said, when no one else spoke. "Tellin' us makes a white man of him, don't it?"

Then he laughed and slapped his knee, looking around at them to see how that sat.

"I already got a grip on all I can lay hand on," he said, and he went off again.

In the hatchway Muller saw the driver move his head to see Wagner better. You could tell he thought himself the only one to joke about the misery of the roadbed.

Then, giving for what he'd got, he said to Wagner, "Get a grip on that billy-goat beard, then, Grandpa."

Then, as Wagner hadn't any answer right off, the driver spoke to them all again.

"We'll be going over stony ground some now. Can't ease it none, sorry to say; you're warned though, at least." Grinning as he was, he had a muskrat look about him. "As best it can, the company aims to please the trade."

"Do tell," the man named Jager spoke up, and about the first time, too. "More travel and less talk would help toward that end."

He didn't say it loud, nor did he seem to have his whole mind on it; he still looked through the window. But the driver heard him clear enough, and pitched his head around *that* way.

"Well, bud, you want I *shouldn't* tell you?"

You might have thought his mouth was full of scallions, it was that bitter. Jager didn't make much of it, though; only kept on looking through the window, as if he cared less for what the driver warned of ahead than he did for what lay behind.

"Tell away," he said, "for all I care. Won't make no difference, anyway."

"Nah, but you'll be feelin' it," the driver said, crowing over it. "You'll be feelin' it soon enough."

For a space it looked like Jager might have more to say, but then he changed his mind and only waved his hand the way you do at something too small to take on over. However, to the driver, this was even worse. Right away his face grew bulgy like the flews of a dog that was ready to

15

bark. Then Lieutenant Patterson spoke up and drew him off before he could reply to the insult.

"This pass here," he said, "is that the one they call Picacho?"

He was looking at a map which he had opened over his knees. He had himself a sack of such maps, and was looking at them all the time, except when he was using them to save his seat. A student of maps, he was.

A little at a time, the driver got his eyes to come away from Jager. His face was still red, however, and grumpy-looking.

"No," he said. "No, it ain't Picacho. Picacho's got a station. It's more north than this, too; twenty mile, maybe. This one's got no name I know of; never heard it, anyhow. Neither did I ever see it on a map. Off and on, though, there's Apaches roosting in it."

You might knew that Wagner couldn't let that go without a comment.

"Then they ought to call it Doubtful Pass," he said. Then he grew more thoughtful while he pulled at his beard. "Come to think of it, seems I got a memory of such a pass, from the old days before the war. More to the south, though."

That was something else he liked to talk about. There was hardly a range of hills they passed by that he didn't know of, or let on he knew about. Muller could have told a few things about this country himself, if he'd minded to; and so he might have if Lieutenant Patterson wasn't along.

"I don't see any pass marked on here," the Lieutenant was saying now. Sure enough, his nose was in his map—a camel nose it was, high and humped up. "It ought to be on *this* one, too. Are you sure there is a pass?"

That got quite a laugh from everyone, and now it was his turn to have a beet-red face. Muller felt it did him good to see that, and he laughed the hardest of them all, except the driver, who nearly lost his seat making up for the hiding he'd got earlier from Jager.

"You want to see my wound, Lieutenant?" The driver's voice came out of him in laughing shouts. "I once sat on an arrow up in that place. You want to *see* it?"

The driver rocked with laughter, and they all were caught up in it once more while Patterson kept getting redder. Nobody thought too much of the Army at that time anyway, and so that added to it. During the war the Army had been taken out of Arizona, leaving it mostly to the Indians. While it wasn't the fault of the soldiers, still it wasn't easy for them now that they were coming through the country again.

But Muller had some reasons of his own, and he was glad to join the others at Patterson's expense.

Only Huston and Miss Hale kept themselves out of it. Miss Hale was trying not to notice what was going on, and Huston only smiled at

Patterson as he might at some child that's had its feelings stepped on. He seemed the kind who would, somehow.

"You know," he said, "the maps are rather vague about the country out here. We haven't had it very long yet. Emory mapped a part of it one time, though. I think Cooke did, too." He leaned across to see it better. "Is this a Cooke map?" he asked.

After the hooting, you could see that Patterson was surprised to find a friend in court. He smiled, moving the map to Huston.

"No," he said, "it's one that Carleton made. General Carleton. I was given a copy at the Point, before I left there."

Huston said, "Ah." Then he said, "Yes, of course; I see it now." He nodded, while he bent over the map; and though he couldn't see much where he was, Muller could have told him that, too. He knew plenty about old Carleton and the California Column; and when that map was laid out, too.

"Well, there you are," Huston said, straightening. "It's fairly new; he went through here in a hurry, if I remember rightly. He was bound to miss some things. No doubt you know that."

"Oh, yes," Patterson said. "Oh, yes, of course."

And *that* he would be sure to know of, brand-new as he was, all spit and polish with his brass still shining. Moreover, he *looked* to be a classroom soldier. There's a way of telling them—something like scent, you might call it. A fellow knows.

"Well, now, have we got it squared away?" the driver said, speaking as he might to women squabbling. "That's nice. Hang on, now, hear?"

And that was all from him. After that, he slammed the hatchway, and while everybody felt around for handholds, Muller heard the driver shouting at the hitch ahead.

Raised on high, his voice was big and brassy, like a bugle sounding a charge in battle.

"Yahoop!" he yelled. "Yahoop! Yahoop!" While over the roof the blacksnake whistled backward, then ahead again until the popper sounded far beyond, like gunshot.

Breaking over their heads, it drove the horses into a lunge against the chains and whiffletrees, so that the whole coach shook and trembled. It shivered that way for a second or two, seeming to hang in balance while the horses heaved and dug at the road. Then it changed; they gradually got the better of the load, and it began to move.

They rolled again, and Muller turned to watch the reach of pallid desert move past the window. Through the window, he could see the dust hang at a higher level than it had earlier—more billowy— and not so flat as when they went faster. Nor did so many stones fly up from the wheels and hoofs, either.

This was mainly a flat that they were going over just now. A little earlier, after leaving Tucson and crossing the Rillito River—if you could call it that—there'd been a rolling country covered over with cholla cactus that rose away toward foothills of the Catalinas standing northeast of town. But now the country had spread out more, and gone flatter, and the cover didn't run so to cholla now. Looking at it, Muller thought how much it differed from the country in New Mexico, and what he had been used to for the past few years. Just the same, he still remembered all this well enough from coming over it with Carleton.

That time it was summer, too, and he had walked across it—not that that made much difference when it came to remembering. Seeing it again, he thought it hardly mattered how he traveled over it, except for comfort. The country was still the same, whether he rode along or marched in a column. It hadn't changed at all—the greasewood and the salt bush, the shine and glitter that made your eyes and head ache, the tawny-hided mountains stabbing through the sand and rock without the gentle round of foothills. The stunted mesquite trees and paloverdes; and the dust and great round heat; a drowning, soaking heat that came from every-where and took you down into it to smother you.

A desert doesn't change much, he thoughlt, watching it move past the window. A desert likes to keep on being the way it always was. In a forest country, a man can leave some sign of having lived in it, or of having been there at least. He can cut the trees and clear the brush away to make a path or a road, and he can build a cabin of the best of what he cuts down; he can clear the ground to plant crops or use as pasture land for his animals. And doing so, he little by little moves the wilderness back.

In a grassland or a valley country, he could do the same thing. Given he had animals, he could graze them there; or, being a farmer, he could plow and sow a furrow to his liking. He could order the country to his needs. In country of that kind, a man could set himself up to be the boss of nature. He could take command of her and turn her workings to his own likes and plans.

In desert country, though, he isn't liable to get so free and easy. Things don't work out quite the way he's used to having them. Out here Nature calls the tune and makes *him* do the dancing. If he's fool enough to try it, or set enough in his mind, he may get by with living in it for a time; but sooner or later, likely, old Mother Nature will have her way with him.

Just let him build a house—one day she'll blow it out from under him. She'll wear it down to a nubbin with sand and grit, or melt it down into the earth from where he got the makings to begin with.

Does he fence in a field and plow it up and plant a crop, she's sure to burn it black no sooner than it sprouts up. Unless he does it the Indian way and plants in little hills to a certain depth; but then no white man of his kind is going to do anything like that.

Even the roads he lays out aren't liable to last for any time, unless he works his body to the bone in order to keep them clear and usable. Just let him turn his back upon them for any time, though, and then the wind is gouging at them, and the run-off flooding them and filling them.

All he sets his hand to one day turns to dust and ashes; and pretty soon, maybe even sooner than he knows it's happening, it's like he never touched it at all.

Just to know that things can happen to him that way makes a man uneasy in his mind; it unsettles him to know such things. No man likes to think that what he makes or builds is liable to be rubbed out, and even forgotten altogether, the minute he looks away. Knowing that he's at the mercy of such a country tells him that he's no account and unimportant in the scheme of things—some different from what he's learned. It makes him know his smallness and his weakness. In a certain way, it's like the stars; they're up there, but he can't do nothing about them. When he finds out he can't organize a place to suit him, he gets afraid of it.

All at once, there, in the middle of that thought, Muller saw himself as such a man. And it didn't matter either that Craig was in a different place than this desert that they were passing through now. It was the same, even so, and did whatever it liked. While it was true that the Rio Grande flowed by the post—too thick to drink, too thin to plow, as they said—you only had to leave it on patrol, and when you hit the barrens you could feel the desert bearing down on you, and have the notion that it's got you, too, and maybe is scheming to keep you for your whole life.

Maybe you couldn't call four years the whole of a man's life, but when you'd served all that time in one place, and had had no leave to break it up, it seemed to be your whole life. He could see it all again, stretching off to doomsday; and he felt it, too, all that world of time and what it was made of: glare, heat, sand and dust since he was first born. Sometimes it had got so he believed he'd never looked at anything without he had to squint his eyes. More than once he'd sworn to God he'd eaten his full weight in sand and rock and dust.

For a moment he drew up, and seemed to see himself that way, fighting and dodging dust. Then his mind moved on and saw the wild red rashes that the dust and heat had made between his toes, behind his knees, and in his elbows and crotch. He still had them, and was ready to believe that he'd had them all his life.

Then there were those letters Helen wrote him from home, back in San Diego. For a long while, they were all that made life bearable at Craig. Reading them, he would be able to hear the breakers on the shoreline down below the Spanish lighthouse, where they used to go for picnics before he joined the Army. He would see the sunlight prancing on the water in the Bay, and see the olive trees and fruit trees sloping toward the mountains.

She liked to write about all those things they'd done together, and how their life would be when he returned home.

Then there was a change. At first, he hardly saw it as a change, but it gradually came over him that her letters were spreading out more than earlier, that they were taking in more territory. They came to mention things he didn't know about, people that he'd never met or even heard of.

Somehow, too, it seemed that she wrote less about the way of things when he came home, after he was mustered out. In some way that was hard to figure, her letters came to be less personal, less intimate. There was hardly a one of these that couldn't be read aloud in the barracks, for all of the little secrets that they had.

And now and then, when writing about their getting married, she even slipped an *if* in there, rather than *when*.

He took that as a joke, but when she brought up

Charley Wilson's name, he could easily tell it wasn't a joke at all, nor any oversight.

He knew Charley Wilson, didn't he? Helen asked him when she mentioned Charley for the first time. Muller knew he'd never heard of anyone of that name before, but Helen made him sound as though he was an old family friend.

Charley Wilson this, it soon came to be; and Charley Wilson that. The name of Charley Wilson came to crawl among the words and lines like lice that had come out of the blanket of a Mescalero Apache at the end of winter. Charley Wilson knew more card tricks than a city gambler, Helen wrote him once. Another time, it turned out, Charley was a great hand when it came to parlor entertainments; he was a tenor. And he had other accomplishments.

Moreover, he was known around as being up and coming in a civic way, and one day he would surely be a pillar of the community. Businesswise, every lady in town was buying her sundries at Charley's counter in the center aisle at Schneider's Mercantile Emporium. It was plain that Mr. Schneider knew it, too, and kept an eye peeled for Charley's advancement.

Anyone could see, she pointed out to Muller, that Charley had a fine head for commerce. And what was more important still, he didn't allow it to get cluttered up with other things. Charley hadn't been so foolish as to go away with General

25

Carleton, halfway across the continent, to fight a war that didn't matter at all to California. Charley was a wiser man than that, and stayed there at home, where he belonged.

Reading that one, Muller felt the desert reaching for him, closing in on him, trapping him. Up to then he'd felt he could make it, like any other soldier, until his time ended. But after she wrote that, he knew something had to be done.

2.

The coach was moving faster by now, and beginning to reach up into the pass. Underneath him Muller felt the roadbed getting rougher, and all of the dust that had rolled in when they had stopped now set up a shaking and shimmering in the sunlight.

Everybody had their grips by now and were holding to the seats beneath them, but the passengers were jiggling as badly as the dust in the air. Up and down they went, the board seats batting at their bottoms, until it felt there were no cushions in between at all.

It was interesting, though, to see the different ways they bounced; each one seemed to have a method of his own. Take Jager, now—he bounced the way a poker might, stiff and jerky, as if to hold himself on guard against whatever came.

Wagner swayed and rolled more than the others did, so that you wondered if his old bones had told him to relax and take it, saying it was foolish to resist. But maybe he was only rump-sprung.

On Muller's side, you couldn't tell too much, it being hard to see directly next to him. It was mostly a smudge of motion made by Huston and Lieutenant Patterson bobbing up and down.

Anyway, the interesting bouncing was across the aisle. Especially did he find Miss Hale's an interesting kind. It was plain she knew it was a thing to draw the eye, because she blushed— though not as much as Helen would.

And one time she caught his glance and looked at him as if to ask him: "Well, Joseph, are you so surprised? You ought to have a pair yourself and take them over the road to California."

But she wasn't able to free her hands in order to settle herself, and could only make the best of things until the road bettered.

From the feel, though, before it bettered it would get still worse. The road was all rock now, the same red stone that had begun to lift around them on both sides; high and steep it was, and many rocks had split off for the coach to bang against as it passed.

And when there weren't the rocks and boulders, there were chuck holes. A mile deep they felt, and every time the coach went into one, that whole side would fly up off the road, and they would bounce along on two wheels while the free ones jibbered on their axles. Then, like as not, another chuck hole would be waiting when they dropped again; and then the other side would fly, too.

Through all this the chance of meeting Indians had left Muller's head, so he was surprised, in one of the times they slammed up out of a hole, to hear Wagner's high shout: "Redskins! Looka there! By hell, it's redskins, sure!"

Muller saw his mouth, a red gap in his beard. He was pointing through the window up the wall of rock, and howling just as wild as any Indian.

Muller tried to see, but when he leaned around the window post to get the angle, there came a sudden sound of driven spikes; and there before his eyes, an arrow quivered in the frame of the door. It was hardly a foot from his head, the stone point come sticking through the wood; and out beyond the frame, he saw the long shaft all atremble to the feathers and nock. It wasn't the first he'd ever seen so close to him, but he could feel his hair pull at his neckline, like any other time he'd seen them do that.

There was something chilling to an arrow; it was different from a ball. You could see them taking root, and you always wondered what it would be like should one come sticking into *you*.

All this came so quick it seemed like a part of the time it took to happen had been skipped over, as if a blank spot in his mind had blocked a part of it. It seemed that hardly a second passed between the time of Wagner's shout, and that of reaching over the grade, the driver yelling, "Yah! Yah!" while the blacksnake popped over their heads. Still, it must have taken more than that, because the pass stretched out for a hundred yards and better, and the coach had only reached it when the arrows started.

The arrow in the frame still quivered with its spent force, when right below it came another one, driving through the panel all the way and putting its war head into the floor. He heard that sound of driven spikes again; he heard shouting, too, this time, a lot of it. At first he thought it must be him who did the yelling, but then it seemed more likely that it came from all of them, because the coach was slamming badly now, and everyone had lost their handholds with the roughness and the burst of speed over the pass.

All of it was run together now, crazy-wild and mixed up, jammed inside the little time it took.

Muller could still hear Wagner shouting about the Indians, and he could see his head half through the window, looking for them while his beard flared up over his face. Once, he caught a glimpse of Jager with a pistol in his hand; and it surprised him that he'd got it out too fast to be seen drawing it. But when he saw him next, the motion of the coach had thrown him down. There he lay, sprawled out on the floor, fighting to gain his feet again.

Over on his shoulder, he could see Lieutenant Patterson wrestling with his own revolver, trying to free it of the scabbard; and it seemed to him that that was *all* he did; that and trample around on top of Jager, who was still down.

He could see Miss Hale a little, too, though it was hard to tell about her in the confusion and dust. But he could see the whiteness of her face, and how the look of her eyes and mouth made it seem that she was less afraid of death than what might happen to her if the Indians should take them alive.

But all of the action was sudden and fast; and things he saw were just impressions, pieces of the whole. It made him think of a deck of cards that, when riffled, will flash the faces so that you can see the colors and maybe even the suit; but the speed is too high to get the sequence.

That was how things went—over the pass and down the far side, the stagecoach slamming, rooting and swaying worse than ever for the boost in speed the grade of the downslope gave it.

Then the coach put a butte between it and the pass, and started yawing. At a bend it started slewing wide across the road and throwing its wheels up. After settling down again, it would cross the road and career up on the other side. It was taken with the wildness of some unnatural creature that denied the driver's will and did the bidding of its own dark mind.

Six or seven times it slewed around and lifted that way, each time wilder than before. Then, all at once, it started rolling; but so slow and easy that he scarcely was aware of it until he looked. Then he saw the rock and sand and small stone rushing up at him through the window.

That was when Patterson shouted, "Ho! We're going over!"

And it was so; they were. What started easy and slow began to go faster. Muller hardly had the time to think about it. All at once he heard the wood smash, and saw the roadway sluicing inward as window and door frames bit in and grabbed. Being on the down side of the coach, he thought to cross his arms before his face; and when he stole a look, it seemed that night had come, for all the sand and dust that clouded out the light of the day. But he could see the dim shape of that camel-faced lieutenant falling his way.

Then he felt the coach slam against the road, drag a distance, bounce partly upright, then hit again and drag solidly. Rock, sand, dust, gravel and stone poured into the breaks. Parts of broken door and window frame came belting around inside; and the passengers were all jammed together against the down side of the coach, with Muller underneath.

• • •

After it seemed the whole side had been torn off, the dragging slowed down, and finally stopped altogether; and when the last of the stone and rock had settled, it grew more quiet. For a moment, then, the only sound came from the up-side wheels, still turning aimlessly on their axles; but they died down slowly while the riders worked loose from each other. For a wonder, nobody had been hurt; but save the careful groping at themselves, they were quiet and round-eyed for a time, the way you are when you've been stunned, say, and still aren't quite sure how things sit.

It was Patterson who came out of it first, and got a grip on things. And that was how it should have been, too, seeing as how he'd had the easy end of it falling on all of them. He'd got his pistol free, too, at long last, and now he was full of business, putting his head up out of the window above him.

Then he saw the arrows in the panels and posts on *that* side, and pulled his head back in.

"We've been attacked!" he said.

Muller had to laugh to hear that high, fluting voice. You'd have thought he'd been skewered himself the way he sounded. Apparently, in fussing with his scabbard in the pass, he hadn't known about the arrows.

Still, it made him laugh and say, "No!"

"You don't think so?" Patterson said. "Have a look yourself, then."

"It happened in the pass," Huston put in. "We're out of it pretty far now; still, I'd be careful."

So Patterson had another look; slower though, and putting only a part of his head up at first. Then he turned around a few times like a prairie dog that's looking the country over.

Then he straightened and said, "It's quiet now. We've lost the animals though. I can't see them anywhere."

"What about the driver?" Huston said.

Patterson had to look some more before he answered again. Now that it was safe, he didn't scrooch any more, but stood up brave and straight.

"Something lying back there," he said after a while. He stretched up on the toes of his polished boots, craning his neck and leaning. "I can't tell too well from here; it's pretty far. It seems to have a human shape, though. It could be him."

"Come on then," Huston said, "we'd better get out there."

So they pulled themselves together and started climbing through the doorway above them. One by one they went up; Patterson going first, as he was partly out already; then Huston; then Muller and Jager boosting Wagner out. The girl was last, with Muller and Jager raising her by her arms, rather than boosting from underneath, because of her skirts.

Then, except for Miss Hale, who stayed beside the coach, they trailed off down the roadway to see what Patterson thought might be the driver.

And it was the driver. He lay sprawled and broken in a part of the roadway where the coach had been dragging. He was lying on his stomach, bent and flattened in a way that told you he'd been ground under it. Muller looked at him the first time full-on, then a little at a time. But it didn't make any difference. He was dead, and so it didn't matter how you looked at him. He was finished, and would joke no more about the road or the pass where once he'd sat on an arrow.

"Jimineee!" old Wagner said in his beard, the hole of his mouth smaller this time; but his eyes bugged out again, as when the arrows came flying.

Huston had got down to take the driver's wrist. He didn't hold it long though. Pretty soon he rose again, shaking his head and dusting the knees of his trousers. Muller noticed for the first time how finely made they were, and that they had the color of the mourning dove. Somehow, they seemed to suit him.

"Too bad," Huston said, like they were old friends. "Too bad. Poor devil. It was sudden though."

They stood there in the roadway a space, solemn and not saying anything. It was quiet, and the baking heat came at them from the sky and from the white road. All around them Muller saw the ruins of the coach spread out in lengths of splintered wood, strips of torn canvas, broken spokes, and even a part of the iron railing meant to hold baggage on top. Over a little ways, he saw the hat the driver had worn, battered and smashed in the dust, all out of shape. And a little beyond the hat, he saw the driver's rifle—or the leavings of it, the action busted.

Pretty soon, he saw a spur, too, lying loose; and when he looked and saw the other on the driver's boot, he thought to wonder why in hell should he wear spurs?

The question made a person of the driver, somehow; a person with a quirk that set him off above the ordinary coachhand who had driven them and joked with them. It was queer to think of, and Muller's mind went on to wonder if the driver had a family somewhere—a wife, say, and some kids.

Then Patterson moved his feet and jiggled the bill of his forage cap with his hand. He looked around at them.

"I daresay we'd better bury him."

He jiggled the bill another time. He seemed a little white around the gills at that moment.

Still, Muller couldn't help but think, "Yah, you brand-new Second John, now you're seein' something, ain't you?"

"Yes," Huston said, "we'd better put him under."

"Burials take time," Jager said. "Why not leave him be?"

This didn't sit so good with Patterson, and he looked at Jager up and down along his nose.

"Why, it's only common decency," he said to him.

Jager let his foot go at a piece of stone.

"Decency be damned. We've got no time for decency. It won't keep him from the coyotes, anyway."

"That doesn't make any difference," Patterson said, seeming to draw up taller as he got his moral ground under him. "It's still the Christian thing to do."

"What about those Indians back there?" Jager said. He jabbed his chin at the pass. His chin was narrow; his whole face was narrow and sharp. "Will those Indians give us time to do the Christian thing?"

He was looking at the pass now, and his face seemed even thinner than before, the way he jabbed with it. It was as if the thought of Indians up there only added to his other worries, and maybe weren't the worst of them, either. Time seemed more important than the Indians.

"We'll see them if they come," Huston said, as if he meant to smooth trouble over. "And if they do, we have only the coach for cover."

It came to Muller that Huston was being what you'd call the voice of reason, though he might have said a dirty word, the way it struck all of them. Thoughts of the driver were forced out, when he recalled the fix they were in. It was peculiar, as if the driver being dead, and the sight of all this wreckage, had so filled their minds there was no room for wondering what might come next.

Huston made it all different.

The pass was back a ways, maybe a mile or better; and in between the point where they'd been hit and where they now were there rose the butte around which they'd gone yawing before the coach had gone over. It didn't seem to Muller that the Indians could see them any more, and so they mightn't know about the wreck.

But on the other hand, they might; it was possible; no matter how things looked, the chance was still there.

So it was true what Huston said about the coach. If there was going to be a fight, it was their only cover. No other place around them offered any.

"I doubt they know we're here," Huston said when they had all looked at the pass and let the thought grow in them. "But whether they do or not, there's still time enough. If they do come down, we'll see them."

You could see it wasn't what Jager wanted to hear; but Huston's logic made it hard to argue. After another look at the pass, he sort of hunched his shoulders up by way of showing he'd go along with it.

So, having it settled, they dug the driver into the ground, putting the shallow hole down into the hard caliche with a spade that Wagner had pulled from the wreckage. Huston gathered up the hat and spur and rifle and put them with the driver, who was lying straightened out now, and kind of peaceful-looking, on the tarp that used to cover the baggage in the rear boot. By then the hole that Patterson and Muller had been working on, taking turns with the spade, was deep enough; and rolling the driver up in the tarp, together with those things that seemed to mean the most to him, they lowered him down, and then shoveled the sand and stone down over him until the mound came out of the hole and stood above the level of the nearby earth. On top of that, then, they piled heavy rocks.

But it didn't make any difference to Jager, even so. He had more to say about it, after all.

"That won't keep the vermin out," he said. "Not if they want him bad enough."

He straightened, and then turned and smiled at Patterson, as if he'd had the last word and meant to show his pleasure.

"But maybe it makes Christians of us now, eh?"

Patterson didn't answer Jager. He simply stood there by the fresh grave looking all about him at the desert and the spiny bald mountains. It was as if he saw it all for the first time.

3.

Seeing the young Lieutenant stand that way made Muller guess at his thoughts, and he felt the whole thing coming down on him. All throughout the arrows flying and the crash that followed the wild ride, he hadn't thought beyond the happenings of the moment. But he did now. Whether the Indians came down or not, they had plenty on their hands. Nor was that all; there were his own troubles, too.

It made him feel unnerved, you might say. And when the others had drifted off to look things over, he ambled back to the coach and sat in a piece of shade.

Then he took the bottle from his coat pocket and had a pull. Somehow, the flask had made it through the crash, and now it still remained about three-quarters full—about the only luck all day long.

He drank from it, and then he held it up to look through the brown glass. The color made it hard to see the little specks floating in it; but the liquor didn't taste any different than when he drank it from a cup or a glass. It was still as much like kerosene as ever, and was enough to make him glad he'd never made a real habit of it, like some he knew.

Perhaps it wasn't so awful, anyway, considering

how he used it. In the beginning there were two flasks, and he'd got them from the sutler over at Craig before he took off—in order to pass the time and maybe guard against a loss of nerve. Muleshoe—a name the soldiers gave it—was one way, no matter how little he ordinarily liked it.

Nursed along, the first bottle had lasted as far as Tucson, even counting the help he'd had with it from Wagner, and the snort or two that Huston took. This second was meant to last the rest of the way, and barring what had happened here, it would have. Now it hardly mattered that he nurse it any longer. All things considered, it might be better that he get the benefit of it now.

So he sat there pulling at it now and then. He could see Miss Hale standing with Jager some distance from the rest of them. The others stood in a group, and when he listened he could hear them talking of the kingpin that had broken, of the horses still running, likely, from the fright, and would the Indians come down, or wouldn't they?

Pretty soon old Wagner left them and came over to sit with him. He let himself down slowly, puffing and red in the face, and leaned his head against the coach so that his beard stuck out.

"You look blown, old man," Muller said. "Time you had a drink."

Muller held the bottle out to Wagner, but Wagner shook his head and wouldn't take it.

"Thanks; you keep it, sonny. Don't know as that's the medicine just now. Water'd do me though. It sure is hot."

"Water cask around in back," Muller said, "seein' you're bent on it."

"Not no more, it ain't," Wagner said. "It's busted."

"The driver had a water bottle with him. What about that?"

"We looked for it but couldn't find it," Wagner said, drawing a breath and letting it out in a way that made his beard flutter. "Coming down, it more'n likely shook loose of him. Pretty quick, we're going to need water."

"Maybe," Muller said, although he hadn't thought too much about water so far. In fact, it needled him a little that Wagner harped on water while he offered his hospitality. Wagner hadn't refused before.

Muller tried again, holding the bottle out, but Wagner still refused. Instead, he signed it away with his hand.

"Not for me, sonny," he said. "And, was I you, I'd go mighty light on it, too. We may be sittin' here awhile, and a fellow as spends a long time in the sun with more'n a little of that in him is asking trouble."

"I guess you ain't the only one that's been around the desert," Muller said.

"Ain't sayin' I am," Wagner told him, now

beginning to push to his feet. "You get to my age, you think about them things."

"You ain't the only one around here that does any thinking," Muller said.

"Can't argue that none," Wagner said. "I expect you got your head full, all right. Still, it's how you think that counts; or what you think. We're in a fix, anyway."

He was standing now, his eyes as sharp as a squirrel's, so that Muller felt a little thrill of doubt creeping along his backbone. For a space, he half expected him to go on and say, "I know all about you, Muller; what you done and what's eating you."

But he didn't. He only held him in his bright eye for another moment, and then he turned and went out into the sunlight where the others were staring off at the far mountains. Soon Jager drifted over and joined them, too; and Miss Hale, left standing by herself, took note of the little shade, and walked to the coach.

Sitting down near Muller, she pulled the long pin from her hat and took it off. The hat was wide and floppy, of a wine shade in color. It matched her long dress, which was the same except for little scraps of white lace about her neck and cuffs.

Muller watched her while she fanned herself with her hat. She had a strong jawbone and a fine-looking neck.

"Lord, it's hot," she said. "I'd forgotten it could

be so hot in the open. It's different in town, somehow."

Muller was still watching her, wondering how his Helen would look in such a rig as that worn by Miss Hale; if she'd wear it, which he doubted.

"Yes, it's plenty hot," he said.

"I don't suppose there's any water handy."

"I don't know about any," Muller said. "Old man Wagner said the water cask got busted, and that the driver lost his bottle someplace. I got this though, and you're sure welcome."

That was when he offered her the muleshoe. If she hadn't dressed in that way, he never would have thought of any such thing. But her clothing seemed to say the offer wouldn't offend her, even if she didn't drink.

And he was right; it didn't offend her at all. Of course, she didn't take it, but she didn't act insulted that he'd thought she *might* have taken it. Was it Helen, now, he might even have had his ears boxed. She was good for a little communion wine, but that was about all.

But Miss Hale only kept on fanning with her hat, saying, "Thank you, I don't think I will. But thank you, all the same. It's kind of you to offer it."

She smiled at Muller, a friendly and open smile that showed her white teeth in even lines between her red lips. Not so innocent as Helen's smile, maybe, but an honest one that he liked.

"Oh," he said, "that's all right," not minding at all that she'd refused. "It's only muleshoe, anyway; I doubt you'd like it. I doubt anybody *really* likes it."

"No," she said, "I don't. But I don't think you should drink it, either—this heat and all . . ."

That time her smile told a good deal more about her than he'd guessed at first—even by her clothes. And he liked it even more, because it seemed to say she wasn't making out to be one thing while really being something else. It made him want to ask her about herself—who she was, where she came from and all that, what she knew about the desert, and how come—but another thought took hold of her before he spoke up.

"Ansel says the nearest water is at the Picacho station."

Ansel was the one who was so sour he wouldn't talk to her; but he'd said something about this Picacho, apparently.

"Well, I guess it is," Muller said, beginning to think about it a little now, though it hadn't really caught him up until Wagner had sounded off; there were so many other things to plague his thoughts.

"It's twenty miles or so up there," she said.

"No need to walk it. They'll be sending some-one out to look for us before long, when we don't get there on time."

"Ansel says they won't. He says they haven't

44

the men to spare now, with the war just over a year, and the line beginning to run again. Anyway, he said there's nothing like a real schedule yet nowadays, so how will they know where we are?"

Now there was something else he hadn't thought of; but it was true enough, and he remembered it now. He'd had to wait five hours in Mesilla Valley for the coach, and scared, too, every minute.

He was quiet for a moment while he thought that over. She, too, was quiet, and when he glanced her way again her hat was in her lap, and he could see the tears leak out of her eyes as she brought up her hands to cover them.

It surprised him so, he didn't know what to do right off. A man should have some kind of training, so he'd know the proper thing for such times. Was it Helen, now, he'd wrestle her a little bit to cheer her up; except that Helen never cried, to his knowledge. Helen didn't seem to feel things in a way that made her cry.

He couldn't think of anything to say, either. Had it only been the thought of walking twenty miles, that and Indians who might trouble them, perhaps he could have thought of something. Except for being leery of letting on about it, he might even have told her that he'd walked across this whole desert once, with Carleton.

But there was more to it than just the walking and Indians; he could feel there was more.

So he did the cowardly thing, and made it seem he hadn't noticed her crying. He made it appear that he was caught up in the conversation of the others, standing a few yards out in front of them, still talking.

And he could hear them, too, once he put his mind on what they were saying.

They were speaking of a range of hills that lay off over the desert plain a long ways to the east. They would point at it, or they would nod their heads at it, so as to make you think they passed judgment on it; weighed it in their minds. Then they'd speak to Wagner, and Wagner'd stick his beard at it. Wagner seemed to be in the middle of the talk.

Then, one time, he heard Huston say to Wagner, "How far would you say it is?"

Wagner combed his fingers through his beard, thinking.

"Oh, seven mile, say. Eight maybe."

"And the name again?" Jager said.

"The Tortolitas," Wagner said, "if I ain't forgot."

"We know that," Jager said, "for Christ's sake. The water though; what's the water called?"

"Oh . . ." and then Wagner combed his beard again, and pulled on it, too. "As I remember, it's Tinajas Altas. Tinajas Altas, that's it. A Spanish name. Means high tanks, or the like."

"It sounds familiar," Huston said, "but I believe I heard it in connection with a water hole along

46

the Camino del Diablo, the old Jesuit trail to Yuma."

"Ain't no reason there can't be two," Wagner said. "Ever count all the Antelope Peaks we got here in the Territory?"

"I don't see it on the map," Patterson said, and sure enough, he had a map out there, too. He could hardly turn around without first looking at that map. Still, thinking of it now, Muller couldn't remember any talk of water in those mountains when the Column went through; for all it pained him to share a doubt with Patterson.

"The pass isn't on it, either," Huston said, "and yet we know there is a pass. I would think it possible, at least, that such water exists."

"It's really mostly a seep," Wagner said. "Still, it catches rain, too, in the season. Did before the war, anyway."

"Been a droughty season this year," Jager said, as if he had to borrow trouble, there not yet being enough for him. "Could easy be dry altogether."

"Maybe," Wagner allowed him. "Not no drier'n here though."

That made them all look round about them for a minute, as if they must make sure of what he said. Off to the south, a little white cloud had shaped above the Catalinas, and lay in the sky like a lamb. They watched it for a time, as if they felt that looking hard enough would make it swell and grow black and come to them full of rain. Maybe

47

it *would* rain, too; but on the Catalinas, and not until later.

Then they turned again and looked off toward the Tortolitas.

"Well, now," Patterson said, while little lines formed over his nose that made him look as grave as if it was a diplomatic matter, "can you be certain of its location? You admit you've been out of the country some time."

"That's so," Wagner said. "Been five, six years, anyway, since I was over there. Still, I'm pretty sure about it."

This time Patterson raised his head in a gentle laugh.

"Pretty sure," he said and laughed again. "Well, now, is pretty sure enough for us? We really need more than that, I think. This can be a mighty big decision, and memory can be tricky."

"Agreed," Wagner said, and then he took a breath and put his beard up in Patterson's brisket. "But once a feller's seen the water holes out here, he don't forget them, neither."

About that time, from the tail of his eye, Muller saw Miss Hale dab her eyes a little with her handkerchief. When she put it down, she said, "I'm sorry to be a fool. I didn't mean to embarrass you."

That was when he knew it wasn't any use to keep pretending that he didn't know she'd been crying.

"It's all right," he told her while he smiled at her. "It didn't bother me at all. You go right ahead again, if you like."

"No," she said, "no, I'm all right now. I don't think I'll do it again. But thanks for your invitation."

She was smiling now, her brown eyes wet with tears and shining so that he was at a loss to think he couldn't help her somehow. But he only had the muleshoe, and she'd refused it once.

Still, there was no reason that he shouldn't offer it another time—it being all he had to show he meant well.

And she took it that time, although he knew right off she only meant to please him. But that was even better than if she liked it.

After she'd tipped the bottle up and down, and given it back to him, she said, "Uff."

"I know it's pretty awful," he said. "And maybe not the best thing just now, either. But it's all I got to offer." He laughed then, to see her mouth still puckered over the taste; and a fine mouth it was. "I'd like it to be champagne."

"Now, that would be something, wouldn't it?" she said. "But, considering your thought, I think it's better than champagne, even though it's dangerous out here."

He noticed that time that the edges of her eyes were crinkled when she smiled, and seeing that seemed to make his head lighter inside. Then the thought of the muleshoe being better than champagne—that and where they were—was so outlandish that he laughed out loud; and she laughed with him.

It was just at that moment that Jager turned around and looked at them. Then he stepped away from the men and walked over. Coming up to where they sat against the coach, he took it all in at a glance—the bottle, and how they sat together, laughing as if they'd heard the funniest joke on earth. They stopped laughing.

"Come on," he said to her straight off, "we're pulling out."

Just like that, he said it, as if she was a servant or slave; and when his eyes passed over Muller, they looked so cold and hollow that the sight set him back; and he thought, surprised, "Why, that man's dangerous!"

As if he worked some power upon her, Miss Hale took what Jager said to her, and how he said it. Muller saw her smile go out like a flame on a candle before a draft, but she still took it. Putting on her floppy hat again, she pushed the hatpin through her hair. Then, with no kind of help from Jager, she stood up and smoothed down her dress. All the while she did this, and when she walked off with Jager, Muller tried to think what kind of man he was to talk to her as he had; and then what kind of girl she *really* was to put up with it.

Then, when they'd joined the others out in the

sun, he felt down again. They were getting ready to leave, and Huston hooked his hand at Muller for a come-on; but he didn't move yet.

He kept sitting there on the ground; and when Huston saw he wasn't coming, he walked slowly over and stood above him. Muller noticed that his face was long, and that his gray eyes seemed to know a lot about a man, just by looking. They were sad, too, as if a lot of what they'd seen in their time was unhappy.

"You ought to cork that bottle, son," Huston said the first thing, and the wrong thing, too, as it happened, for all that Muller hadn't touched it since the kind of fix they were in had grown on him. But he was finished taking orders, or anything that sounded like one.

So he said, "Oh? Making you thirsty, am I?"

"No, not at all. Nor am I criticizing you."

Then he smiled, and settling on his haunches, he gave Muller's leg a pat, as if he thought him a boy. He wasn't though; he was twenty, coming twenty-one in August, on the fifteenth.

"But we're going on a walk," Huston went on. "Quite a long one, too, and you'll need your strength. Alcohol and heat don't mix."

It didn't help to know they'd planned a walk for him. No more than have another lecture on the muleshoe.

"Nobody talked to me about any walk," he said.

"Consider yourself invited then," Huston said,

with another smile. "We're going for water over there in those mountains."

He turned, lifting his arm to point off through the heat haze toward the far, crouched shapes; but Muller hardly looked at them. He was going to make his own plans for a change. Huston wouldn't buy him off as easy as that. And, anyway, he'd never heard of water in those mountains while marching through here before. Then they had had their canteens, with water casks on the wagons.

"What's the matter with staying here?" he said.

"For one thing, no water. For another, those Indians could still come down. Either way, to stay is taking a chance."

Muller knew that, too, but still he felt sore. It was all a part of the feeling he'd had since pulling out of Craig. Even so, with Huston as the voice of reason again, he might have given in, if only Patterson and Wagner had kept out of it.

But they didn't. They, too, came over; and after Huston spoke to them, they were bound to have their say.

"Come on, there, Muller," Wagner said. "No pay dirt here." Smiling, he gave his head a little jerk.

"Don't be a fool," the Lieutenant said. "We've got to reach water."

When Patterson sounded off, that's what changed his mind. It was just what Muller'd shook free of, and he'd be damned if he'd take it from any green West Point shavetail.

"Go on to water, then," he said. "Given you find it; I ain't stopping you."

"Have it your way," Patterson said, and having done his duty as he saw it, turned away. "Are we ready?" he asked the others.

"Ready as we can get," Wagner said. He shook his head at Muller again; a real shake, it was, this time.

"You two shove off," Huston told them. "I'll be right along."

"All right, but hurry," Patterson said.

They turned away, and when they reached Jager and Miss Hale, Muller saw her look around at him—as if she'd like to urge him to come, herself, but daren't. It pleased him that she might have thought of asking him, but he still sat, a little befuddled by the liquor and his private troubles.

Then Huston took the derringer from his waistcoat and held it out. "Take it, if you don't mind, son. You may need it before long."

"Thanks," Muller said; and then, all at once, he felt ashamed of how he'd talked to Huston before. "Thanks, just the same. I got one somewhere in the boot, with my gear."

"All right." Huston put it back in his pocket. "You're welcome to it, however." He leaned over, reaching for Muller's hand and shaking it gently.

"Good luck to you, boy. I wish you'd come; but your troubles are your own business."

"Thanks again," Muller said. "Good luck to you, too."

And he meant it; for no matter how he felt about the others, how he felt about this whole thing, right from the moment it started, he liked Huston.

Then Huston joined the others, and all five, saving Jager, waved. As they started off, Muller saw Miss Hale look back at him over her shoulder, but she wasn't smiling this time. The Lieutenant's boots were shining in the sunlight, and Muller knew the young officer would soon be wishing that he'd never seen those boots.

For a moment, thinking that, he felt better. Then it changed, because the rest was bad and already he could feel the loneliness, and the muleshoe heating him up. All of his schemes and plans had gone sour; it didn't do any good any longer to tell himself that he'd been right in busting out of Craig because they wouldn't give him leave. And it didn't do any good to keep on telling himself that Helen would be waiting, either, like he'd done all along.

Maybe she would be waiting, but she'd written that she'd been asked by Charley Wilson, too—so maybe she wouldn't be. Deep down, he guessed he'd known that what she'd said was more than a simple threat, or an urging to action.

He could tell himself those things before,

however; make out that everything would be all right, and get away with it—believe them even. He could when they were moving, getting there. But now with this happening, and the loneliness growing, it all changed.

And now he knew he'd be a fool to go to muleshoe for cheer. In fact, had he known this was coming, he'd never have brought it along, even though there was small danger in it while riding.

All at once he knew he couldn't stay there alone. His mind seemed to change before he knew it. But all at once, sitting by the wreckage, he felt the bigness and emptiness, with the desert too wide and stretching out into nothing. It was better to be with others, and no matter he'd never heard of those water holes Wagner mentioned. Facing the facts he knew this was his only chance, and he wasn't about to quit, however things had turned and twisted for him. Even if you die, it's better in company.

Of a sudden then, he got up and shouted, "Wait! Wait! I'm coming!"—throwing up his arms.

They turned, but slowly, as if already saving strength, and when he knew they'd wait he went around to the boot to get his pistol and cartridges. The broken water cask had soaked most everything, but his revolver, together with the primers and paper cartridges, had got only a little damp. He put them in his coat pocket, wrapping the cartridges and primers in his handkerchief, in order not to lose them while walking.

That was all he took of his things, except his Army paybook. That was more than just damp—the leaves were wet and limp, and some of the writing had turned runny; but the look of it didn't matter. He took it just the same; after all, he'd taken it this far, and now it somehow meant more. It was the having it that mattered. Maybe you can't let go as easy as you think you can.

He took the flask of liquor from his pocket, looked at it a moment, then stooped and broke it on a rock, letting what was left trickle into the sand. Maybe they were right about it, after all, he thought, if they were going to have to walk in this desert heat.

4.

Maggie turned her back upon the coach a last time, and with the others, set out over the desert toward the mountains that Wagner said would hold water for them. They walked across the hot ground by twos, being careful that they keep a space between each pair, so that they wouldn't bunch, or stumble on each other's heels. Doing it that way was a notion of Lieutenant Patterson's, and it worked out well enough, although it seemed to have a military flavor.

Up at the head of the line, in front, the old man trudged along beside Lieutenant Patterson. Behind them by a few yards came poor Joseph, next to Huston, who seemed disposed to keep an eye out for him.

She and Ansel came along at the end of the line. Ansel made the choice. He always said it made him nervous to be surrounded, and preferred a place where he could have a view of what happened.

Starting out, they went on steadily, but slowly, taking care to hoard their strength against the long hours ahead. As Wagner'd said—and she was better off believing him than not—they'd need most of the afternoon to cross over; and going easily would be more comfortable than if they hurried along.

Comfortable: that was how he put it. And Maggie nearly laughed to think of being comfortable out here. Wagner might know plenty about the country, and the way to water, too. But what he knew about the suitability of women's wear for traipsing over the broiling desert was something else. Even Ansel would know better than to say that. But, come to think of it, he ought to.

Anyway, right then and there, it was enough to peg old Wagner as a woman-shy bachelor.

The main thing wasn't a matter of comfort anyway. It was endurance. It was being able to hold your feet and keep moving.

She supposed she could at least be thankful for having reasonably level ground to walk on. Soon enough she found that it was littered with a million burning stones, and every one of them seemed bent on poking through her shoes which, as their soles were thin, made stepping on the really sharp ones like walking along barefoot. The floppy hat brim served to shield her face against the sun, but it did little for the rest of her. And underneath her petticoats, she soon began to feel the rivers of perspiration running down. It was hot beneath her bodice, too, a thing that made her envy the men the looseness of their shirts. Still, it wasn't just the cut of the cloth that made her bodice so tight; but then she couldn't help the way her body had grown.

For a while, when they'd got started, she watched the mountains out ahead in order to see if they were coming nearer, and trying to guess what part of them might hold the spring, or seep, or whatever it was that Wagner was taking them to.

But it wasn't long before the effort wearied her, and she gave it up. The glare of earth and sky was too harsh.

It wasn't long before it was enough for her to watch her feet, anyway. It didn't make any difference that she'd lived in Tucson for a year and more, she didn't have much feeling for the desert. Except in springtime, when its harshness softened for a moment with the spate of cactus blooms and wild flowers, she never felt any call to look at it. For her, it seemed to wear a lonely face; and there was something cold or withdrawn about it, too; a place that was withheld from your knowing much of it. Somehow, it seemed almost secretive, and gave a feeling of living only to itself and for itself. Then there were the lizards and snakes.

Thinking of it, she grew full of wariness. She glanced about her into the web of shadows which the greasewood cast upon the hot earth. In the second of shifting her glance, her eyes passed over the stone that lay beyond her, and coming forward for the next step, her foot came down upon it. First, the sharpness pressing at her thin sole broke her stride. Then she lost her balance and began to fall over; but, in throwing out her arms, one of them struck Ansel and he turned in time and jerked her back up.

As she steadied again, he let her arm drop down.

"You've got to watch it," he said.

"I'm sorry," Maggie said, knowing his manner faulted her, and that she had to apologize. She could always tell.

"You've got to watch it," he said again. "You've got to watch your feet."

"I'm being as careful as I can, Ans," she said. "Sometimes it's hard to see, though. The glare's so sharp." Ansel wouldn't show her any mercy for her worry over lizards in his mood today. It was better to blame something else.

"Maybe that bottle had some glare in it," he said.

"Maybe, but I wouldn't know it," Maggie said. "I hardly tasted it, and didn't like it any."

She glanced at him, trying to read what might be in his mind, although she'd never had much luck doing that. Likely she should have mentioned the lizard, after all.

"You know that," she added while she watched him for a sign of some kind. "You know I never liked it at Rodriguez's, either."

"You didn't seem to mind it back there, at the coach."

She knew his mind now, all right. And it was strange how he could disregard her so long, and yet show his streak of venom when she passed a word with some other man.

But, as had become her way, she felt defensive before him.

"Oh, Ansel, I was only trying to please him a little bit; what's wrong with that? He seems so lonesome, somehow. How could that hurt anything?"

"Seems it hurt your eyesight some," Ansel said. He was smiling now, she saw, but in that way that she had come to know so well.

"Not that little bit I tasted," she said; and now, all at once, she felt degraded that she must apologize for sitting with Joseph. It was as if she daren't draw a breath without having permission from Ansel first.

Then, knowing that fanned up an anger in her, and she stamped her foot.

"At least he talked to me!" she said. "And he was glad enough to have me talk with him, too!"

"I noticed that," Ansel said, looking straight ahead now. His grin was gone.

"Yes," she said. "That's more than *you* can say, Ansel!"

Ansel turned his head and smiled.

"I'm talking to you now."

"How gracious of you! Crumbs for the poor from the plate of the master! And what about the coach? What happened to your kindness then?"

"Talk, talk, talk. Why should I talk all of the time? Once in a while I like to think. And, anyway, you gab enough for us both."

These days it sometimes seemed to Maggie that all they did was quarrel with each other. But even quarreling with Ansel could be better than his long, brooding silences. To her thinking, loneliness was kin to silence, and she feared and hated them both.

"Ah," she said, "perhaps his lordship had his mind on state matters. Perhaps he had it on Rodriguez?"

"Maybe he didn't, too," Ansel said, but his answer lagged enough to tell her that she'd been right, and she went on after it.

"Perhaps his lordship's mind was busy with the cards then," she said. "Maybe thinking of other ways to mark them."

She had crossed a line there, and the knowledge filled her with a strange kind of elation. Ordinarily she never talked about his gambling methods; only the money his endless gambling cost her.

"I'd forget about those cards, if I was you," Ansel said. "I'd forget about Rodriguez, too."

"Forget about Rodriguez? Why, Ansel? You may remember that I had a good job with Rodriguez. It fed me at least, and fed you more than once, too. Until you spoiled it for me with your stupid tricks."

On saying that, she drew up and waited for his rage. But he didn't reply. Rarely did she dare to taunt him for his follies, and now his failure to react made her still bolder. It was the wearing of the heat, the feeling of lostness riding her—here and every place—and the knowing that she loved him with a vain, prideless love. These things, coming all together in her mind at one time, spurred her tongue.

She drew a breath and let it out in a rush.

"Cheat!" she cried out. "Common cheat! Common, greedy cheat!"

Then, no sooner had the awful words burst loose than her hand raced up to her mouth, and her mind went half numb with fright.

"Oh, Ans," she said, "oh, Ans, I'm sorry. I didn't mean to say that; honestly, I didn't. I didn't mean a bit of it."

While she spoke, she touched him, but he pulled his arm back. Then she ran ahead of him a few steps, trying to catch his cold eye, but he wouldn't look at her and only stared out on the glitter of the desert and kept silent.

She gave it up at last, and like a dog that has been called to heel, fell back beside him, knowing it was no use to plead. She knew the signs, as it was something that he'd done to her before, often enough. Whenever he was angry with her over something that she'd done, or something that he'd imagined she'd done, he wouldn't speak to her or notice her. Knowing how to use her love for him, Ansel long ago had found the way to punish her for things she did, or didn't do, that he didn't like. In giving herself to Ansel, Maggie knew he understood the emptiness of her life without him. Being a solitary man, Ansel knew what loneliness could mean to other people, and how to use it as a weapon for his own ends.

Coming down to it, she thought, it ought to be the other way around; or anyway, what passed between a man and a woman ought to be more equal—not something so lopsided. A woman, in particular, needed to be desired beyond the physical demands that men made upon her. In order that she be fulfilled and live as Nature had in mind that she live, she required to be needed for all the values given her; not only those that frolicked about in Ansel's mind.

She was like a little plant that must be nourished with the knowledge of her meaning to the happiness of others. A woman had to be appreciated in order that her nature might be fulfilled.

Granted that, she thrived and spread herself; knowing she was loved and needed, she would not complain of life. But when that knowledge was denied her, life became a pointless thing without a purpose of any kind.

Anyway, that was how it seemed; her instincts and her secret little inner knowings told her that. And while she'd never known the lasting love or need of any man to give her life that proper fullness, she had enough experience to know its barrenness without those things. There was little barrenness of which she hadn't bitter knowledge.

It had been different at the start. At least, it had seemed different, although the other girls with whom she had been working at Rodriguez's had said that, in the long run, Ansel would be a troublemaker.

A look, they'd said he had; the kind of look a scalpman had, hunting hide.

And maybe it was true, too, though at the time she'd laid such talk to jealousy on their part; and by their lights, they did have cause for jealousy. For, as a rule, wherever she found work she seemed to have a quality of girlish innocence that made her useful as an ornament, someone who was able to give the establishment some tone.

As Rodriguez himself had told her when she'd come to Tucson and the Apex, "One can always find a riding horse without much trouble; but one to prance?"

That was how it happened that she wasn't required for entertainment out in the private rooms, away from the main bar. The other girls might be called upon to wallow in their sweaty beds with soldiers on leave from McDowell or Grant or Bowie; with the miners down from long months in the hills; with wagon freighters passing through town (most of them wore red underwear, and such a sight); or with the filthy scalpmen who came down the Santa Cruz from Mexico, the hides of Indians at their bloody belts; or, if not the hides, then the money paid them by Sonora and Chihuahua, as bounty.

But as her place was in the main bar, where it fell to her to keep the gaming mood inviting and happy, she managed to keep a cut above the other girls. So you could hardly blame them much for jealous talk.

All the same, maybe it was true about Ansel's look. Surely, he was different from any other man she'd known before he happened along. Nor was it look alone that did it. For a fact, he seemed to be all ice and fire, and the strange thing of it was that, even at first, he developed little fears inside of her.

But she was drawn to him much more than warned off. Something in her found it thrilly to have a man so smoky-looking and intense as he was, making over her, saying things that might be taken as a joke, or again, maybe not, depending. Things to make you blush, or ought to. Pressing your hand a little harder than was needed, for a greeting. Breathing at you. And later on, making love so as to stop your breath and make your skin rise up prickly and chilled.

In those days he was tender and exciting, both; always ready with a sly remark or with a smile turned so upon a word that you would wonder at its meaning, and would long for more. If he had any danger in him then, it would be the kind that drew a spirited girl.

But that was long ago; and in between what she had come to think of as a youthful time of gay hope, and this of trailing over the shaking plain, there lay those dark days of disillusion: his endless hours at the tables; the loans she made him from her pay—gifts, in fact; her protests that he gambled away her earnings; and his spleenful rages at her critical talk.

Then, when he began to win at last, the telltale

softness of his sanded finger tips on her flesh—she knew his touch so well by that time; the cards that had been razored, or changed elsewise; until finally, to bring a sorry end to it all, Rodriguez's lidded glance upon Ansel, and upon herself, too. After all, she'd banked his game.

Now in the roaring heat, a part of her mind stood off to ask if she shouldn't have cut free of him long ago and have done with him.

Surely, the part of her mind that asked was speaking out of good sense, to say nothing of propriety. Though propriety was something that she hadn't thought of too much lately.

But then that other part of her mind, whose wayward bidding she had done most often, despite the early warnings, had said to follow Ansel away.

And she had, although she knew by now that nothing good could come of it. Nor had he wanted her to come with him, either; the sulk he'd worn since early morning, when she'd surprised him at the station, showed that. Such love as he might show for her these days was only an animal rutting, a passing lust that had no content for her heart whatever.

Still she sought it out, and was grateful for its fevered moments, degrading though she knew it to be. In her emptiness, his spells of panting, swarming passion were all that kept despair and loneliness away from her.

5.

It was some later now; and as the sun scorched across the milk sky of summer, it began to sneak beneath the brim of Maggie's hat and lay its bright heat on her face and neck. She couldn't begin to think how far or for how long they'd traveled, but whenever they rested, the Lieutenant would have a figure worked out for them. He arrived at this in some mysterious manner that was too involved for Maggie to follow, though she tried to at first. But it didn't seem to make much sense to her, and after getting the distance all turned around a couple of times, she felt so low in her mind that she stopped listening.

In fact, it might be better *not* to know how far they'd come. It always seemed to turn out less than what she'd thought. Just when she had reached the point of thinking that she could go no farther, and that surely they would be there soon, then Lieutenant Patterson would tell them that they'd come only a third or a quarter of the way. And to learn that what remained was even more than that already made would make her body groan all over.

This particular time, before they'd made much more than halfway, fixed itself in her memory as the time of the arguments. It wasn't she who argued; it was the men. Their being in a tight, it seemed that quarreling and the bellowing of opinions was all a part of getting out of their trouble. Or maybe it served to ease their feelings. Being men, of course, it wasn't only their fix they argued about; men quarreled about the silliest things.

The first argument was over the Indians. The men were sprawling in some tattered mesquite shade, resting, and Lieutenant Patterson was putting his watch away and looking off at the pass.

"Anything back there yet?" Mr. Huston asked him.

"No, I see nothing," the Lieutenant answered. "We got away from them, all right. They no doubt think we're well along toward Picacho by now."

"I wouldn't be too sure of that," Joseph said.

"What d'you mean, you wouldn't be too sure?" the Lieutenant said. "I should think it's obvious. They're surely not in sight out there."

"That doesn't mean much," Joseph said. "That's the time to be most scared of them."

"Out here? As wide open as this is?"

"Uh-huh," Joseph said. "That's the time."

"Why, that's childish," the Lieutenant said. "That's like being afraid of ghosts."

It was plain to see that Joseph didn't like that very well, and he began to push up on his elbows, but Mr. Huston spoke then.

"Not exactly," he said. "They have a way of showing up quite suddenly, wholly unannounced."

Otto Wagner now got into it for the first time.

"Even quicker'n that," he said. "For a fact, they come right out'n the earth at your feet. I seen 'em do it."

"Now, really," the Lieutenant said, smiling. "I find that incredible. You can't ask me to believe that."

"That pass sure slipped your mind quick," Joseph said.

"We're not talking about the pass," the Lieutenant said. "We're talking about out here, in open ground. Maybe yes, in ambush, but not out here. We could see their every move. They wouldn't have had the time to catch us, anyway. Our starting point was well ahead of where theirs would be."

It was now that they began to veer away from the main point of discussion, and start pushing a little at one another. It was Joseph who set it off, seeming driven to it somehow.

"There's another thing you're all wet on," he said.

"I beg your pardon," Lieutenant Patterson said.

"He means you're talkin' through your shako," old Wagner said.

This brought Mr. Huston edging in a little closer, as if he meant to get them back upon the main trail again.

"They could have horses," he said. "Although we certainly would see horses."

"They could catch us easy enough without horses," Wagner said. "Apache bucks, in good shape, can make a hundred miles a day and better, on foot."

This time Lieutenant Patterson laughed out loud. "Oh, my God!" he said. "What do you take me for?"

"As a matter of fact," Mr. Huston said, "that is a bit long."

"Yair?" Wagner said, turning and poking his beard at Mr. Huston. "I been in this country before, I guess."

"Uh-huh, an' got your redskins mixed up," Joseph said.

Wagner turned and pushed his beard at Joseph now.

"How do you mean that, boy?"

"Only that Apaches don't peel it off like that," Joseph said. "It's Hopis. Driven, a Hopi runner can go a hundred and twenty if he has to. Apaches do good to make seventy-five; Tonto, Chiricahua, Pinal, whatever; it don't make any difference."

Everybody looked at Joseph now, kind of squinting at him, as if they had to think before saying anything more.

Then the Lieutenant said, "Where did you ever hear that?"

"Well, it's not too far off," Huston said, like he might know a little, too.

It was plain that Wagner didn't think so much of this talk, as he was still ruffled. "For a kid as ain't said much until now, you're sure gabby," he said.

"I just like to see things truthful," Joseph said. "And I ain't no kid, either."

"Just a kid giving the facts of life to grandpa," Ansel put in to make it plain he meant to get into the argument, however far he might be from the main point. And by now every one of them was pretty near as far away as they could get. Right away they jumped on Ansel, who deserved it, seeing as he'd asked for it.

"Who asked you into it?" Joseph said.

"You sayin' I ain't got a right to talk?" Ansel said right back at him.

"Since you are, then," Wagner said, "you mind saying who that grandpa was you just mentioned?"

"Men, men," Lieutenant Patterson said, "this has no bearing on the matter." He put his hands in the air. "Please, please. This is getting disorderly."

He was right, of course, it was. But rather than quiet them down, his drill-ground tone just made them noisier. They waved their arms at him and shouted, asking who was getting disorderly? And Joseph, in particular, said that he'd be god-damned if he'd be taking any order from him.

Then when it appeared that Joseph and Lieutenant Patterson might get even more dis-orderly, Mr. Huston stood and said, "Gentlemen, gentlemen, please! We can't squander our strength in this way." He waved his arm at the faraway mountains and went on, "That's where it must be spent, in reaching that."

That ended it, all right, with all of them falling quiet and kind of drawing in while they looked —what Maggie came to think of as the Indian argument; although it only started out with Indians, and as with any other male quarrel, settled on personalities.

A little later another one came up; or perhaps it wasn't a little later, but much later. Time was strange now in its passing, and the places where they rested were becoming vague in order and number.

One time they made a stop beneath a paloverde, but because it had no true leaves—only greenish spines—it did little to screen the solid pounding of the white sunlight. Another few times they sought out shade in low greasewood patches.

Once, or maybe it was more than that, the Lieutenant made a show of scouting through the cover in advance, in order to scare off any rattle-snakes or lizards or little pack rats that might have crawled in ahead of them. But these efforts didn't last long; and he gave it up in time, as if it didn't matter very much anyway.

And maybe it didn't matter too much, either, any more; for Maggie gave hardly a thought to the one and only lizard that *did* catch her eye—a little gheko that went running off in wild panic.

It was as if those things of which she once had been fearful had lost their meaning, or had been replaced by those which she could never have known until she faced them.

You could never imagine such a heat as this; nor such a weight of weariness, until they happened to you. And once they had, why, lizards were a joke.

They were hunched against the bottom of an ocotillo when the cloud talk began. Past blooming time, the fringe of red petals on the skinny stalks had long since blown off, the small green leaves gone papery and brown in the great summer heat. Not that it would have made much difference if they hadn't. Ocotillos only offered shelter at their bottoms anyway.

But it was all there was at hand, and she was glad enough to flop beneath it for the few moments they allowed themselves.

Sitting there, she fanned herself with her hat, holding her bodice out with one hand and scooping the air in with the wide brim, while more than ever she wished she were a man, and so be able to lie there with her coat off and her shirt open.

That was how they lay now, most of them, like panting hounds. Only Ansel and Lieutenant Patterson had their coats on. Maybe the Lieutenant, as an officer, considered it improper to be seen in shirt sleeves, but Ansel had no good reason not to.

It even angered her a little that he sat there seeming not to mind the heat, while she stifled in her tormenting bindings.

"You ought to take off your coat, Ansel," she said. "Aren't you hot?"

"I don't mind it on," Ansel said.

"You're going to cook that way."

"That's all in the head. The more you think of it, the hotter it gets."

"Maybe that works for you," Maggie said, "but I'd give anything to take this dress off."

"Go ahead," Ansel said, smiling now; then his glance moved over the other men. When his eyes came back to her, the grin grew wider. "What's keeping you?"

She didn't answer that, but turned away from him, feeling lost and sick. On her other side, Joseph watched her, smiling at her, too; though not as if he'd heard Ansel. Just pleasant, as when they'd sat together at the coach.

"Tell you what," he said, "I'll fan awhile, if you like."

It was good to laugh again, and she wondered if he meant it or was just joking. Likely it was best to treat it as a joke, for all she didn't care just now what Ansel might think.

"Thanks, but I don't mind it," she said. "You'd only get hotter doing it."

"I wouldn't care," he said. "I wouldn't mind at all."

75

That was when Ansel leaned across to scowl at her, and at Joseph, too; but before he spoke, if he was going to speak, the Lieutenant rose and pointed at the cloud above the Catalinas.

"What about that cloud?" he said. "Do you think there's any rain in it?"

No one spoke at first, as he hadn't asked of anyone special. Then Mr. Huston said, "Could be. Not much yet though. Later on there ought to be some. It's the regular time for summer rains."

"Why, I don't know," Joseph turned and said to him. "I've seen it rain at other times in the summer."

"Oh, it happens," Mr. Huston said. "I've seen it, too. In general, though, they start in late afternoon. There must be a chance for thermal development."

Whatever that was, Maggie thought.

"Well, allowing that it does rain," the Lieutenant said, "is it likely to reach us here?"

"A good question," Huston said. "It's dependent on the airs. A local storm, most likely; they usually are. Anyway we can't tell yet."

Ansel had to have his say then. So long as what he said was disagreeable, he could break his silence. Had he not spoke up, there might not have been a cloud argument at all.

"I can't see it makes much difference either way," he said. "Our water hole's still out there, isn't it?"

"That's the supposition," the Lieutenant said.

That stirred Wagner up again, of course. "What d'you mean by that?" he said.

"What he means," Joseph said ahead of the Lieutenant, "is if it ain't on his map, it just ain't anywhere."

The Lieutenant turned on Joseph then, and it was funny how the angriest part of the quarreling seemed to fall between those two. Though Ansel had baited the hook, you might say.

"You seem to know a lot about my maps, for a civilian," he said.

"I might know more'n you think I do," Joseph answered.

Hearing that, it was another time when everybody looked at him; especially Mr. Huston, who looked at him the hardest, except for the Lieutenant, who already watched him.

"I doubt that," the Lieutenant said in a moment. "If you did, you'd also know it to be fairly accurate. Save some odds and ends, it shows the country's features quite well."

"Odds and ends," Joseph said, turning to Wagner, "that's a good name for your spring, isn't it?"

"I didn't call it that," the Lieutenant said.

"Lord to God, man, we all heard you!" Joseph said.

"I was only speaking in a general way, that's all. I simply used the term to cover all omissions on the map."

"I guess that means the spring, all right," Joseph said.

"God bless it, I said nothing about that spring, Muller! Not one word have I said about it!" He came nearer Joseph and his voice went higher as he stood above him. "And I'll thank you not to put words in my mouth. That doesn't help things any! You don't have to come with us, if you don't like how things go!"

"I guess I got a right to go where I please," Joseph said, becoming angry himself now. There was something of an odd look about his eyes and forehead, Maggie noticed; as though the heat was showing, or the muleshoe. Unless the Lieutenant was in back of it somehow; that could be.

"A pity it didn't please you to stay at the coach, the way you wished to in the first place," the Lieutenant said.

Except that Mr. Huston calmed them down again, there might have been more. You could say the arguing was the same as last time, except that they brawled sooner, and that the really angry part was between Lieutenant Patterson and Joseph. So far as Maggie knew, they were total strangers, yet they niggled at each other like old enemies—especially Joseph, for whom the need to quarrel seemed more important than what was quarreled about. Surely, she thought, something was bothering him which would give him no peace.

While she wondered what that was, it didn't
make much real difference; she felt drawn to him
in any event. She knew trouble when she saw it,
and that was enough. Knowing they had something of the same thing inside them made it hard
to be put out with him.

After that the arguments grew shorter and
fewer, and were mostly over fidgety little things
like the ground they'd covered and what might
be left. They were finding it was true what Mr.
Huston said, that they didn't have the wind to
quarrel, as well as make their way across the
plain to the mountains.

6.

She was walking slower now, just dragging, it
seemed. She could feel the jarring of the ground
more, with every step a blow that punished her
legs and spine. She could feel a scalding fire in
her shoulders. Her feet were getting to be like
slabs of fried meat; the soles were scorched, and
the toes and ankles cringed against the hot
leather.

The fine dress that she liked so well, that
showed her figure to its best advantage, was a
ruin of sweat and wrinkles; and there was even a
rent or two from going head over heels when
the coach had spilled. She could feel the clinging

wet against her back and in her armpits. All along the front, the bombazine was stained, the outline of the dark puddles showing white with salt rime.

She must have sweat a gallon so far, and the end was not yet. She would be smelling ripe by now, too.

How cruel it all was, she thought—thought it as it might be thought by someone who had known her before her beauty became a shambles; before her clothes had reached this sodden, drab condition; before her handy figure had wilted and her fair face had gone slack and dull and old. While all about her there stretched the plains of bright fire, the naked, smoking hills, and, at a far reach of the eye, the aimless, drifting dust devils—lost souls of Apache dead, they called them—the shuddering haze of heat; as if it were a landscape from hell.

Hell! The word flared in her mind, and all at once her thoughts went spinning backward to another time and place. They swept her to New York, and she was talking to her mother in the shoddy room where they lived.

The war was at an end, and she was taken with the sense of change that seized the country. All about her were the gray and sameness of the slums, the petty meanness and the brutish violence of the squalid, dark streets; and she was brimming with a zest to taste the life she winded on the new, restless air.

"West!" her mother said, and threw her hands up. "Oh!"

"But, Ma, lots of folks are going west nowadays," Maggie told her. "Now the country is safe for travel. You only got to look around you to know, Ma."

But Ma had never looked around her much, having lived her life within a few square miles of being born and settling down to marriage and her own family. Among them, only Pa—God rest and keep his gay soul—had traveled, and knew what far-off horizons could mean. Pa had been an Ulsterman; he had come across the water in his brash youth, and Maggie still recalled the wild tales of green Irish hills spinning from his lilting tongue. Some said inheritance had given her the lilt, too.

"Only sluts and murderers go west," Ma declared, "if it's the truth you're after."

She started crying then, her old apron at her face, and Maggie saw her knuckles red and rough against the white cloth.

"Look about yourself, Maggie," she went on between the sobs that shook her thin shoulders. "Look at Bridgett, if you don't mind. Why can't you take factory work, too? You've always had a fine touch with drawn things."

"No, no," Maggie said, and she could hardly stand the thought of more factory work. During the war, when doing piecework on Army uniforms, she'd had her fill of that life: the fidgety repetition, her pretty tapered fingers pricked and sore and reddened. Even now, she was able to feel her buttocks where the foreman squeezed them when he passed her bench, or stood behind her while he made out to inspect her stitch or the quality of the cloth. When it came to that, no common factory hand would be her choice to do such squeezing as she might allow.

"No!" she said in a fright. "No, I want to be free! I want to be free to follow the sun!"

"The sun!" Ma cried. "Oh!" And when her apron fell, it was as though an old grievance had come to life in her mind.

"Oh!" she cried again. "I swear your father speaks in you, girl!" She put her finger up in Maggie's face and worked it back and forth. "Wander, wander, follow the sun—I've heard him say those very words. Oh, the ruin of it! Now to find the black blood of his wanderlusting running in you!"

"It's your blood, too, Ma," Maggie said. "Don't forget that."

"Not the wandering part, girl! Nor the part that lusts for what I can't begin to think of, either. But, by all the signs, still lusts. Not the restlessness, the wantonness!" Her finger worked again in Maggie's face. "Bless God, it is the sinners and sluts that heed the call of the devil, girl! And it's straight through hell's gate that he'll be taking you, too!"

Now, dear God in heaven, had it all come to pass? Was this grimly ashen wilderness the hell to which she had been doomed to wander for her dreadful sins and her depraved life? Was this that somber day of retribution and atonement?

Her eye passed over the pallid, brown plain; the outlandish growths of thorns and claws that crouched in alien shape ahead of her, as if lying in wait to grasp her as she went by; the heat waves rising through the jellied air above the desert and the bald hills and mountains.

Through the tears that blurred her vision, the glare was fractured, and then broken into planes as through a prism; so that she suddenly beheld the livid, glistering blue of brimstone, hellfire's sulphurous yellows and greens, the monstrous reds of lava flowing in rivers of fire across the floor of the desert.

From far, far off, she could hear her mother's voice.

Then she heard another, coming from her memories of childhood. It was very old, but it was clear, too, and she could even smell the musty odor of the confessional while the priest spoke in his dim wispy voice. He was shriving her of girlish follies; but he was warning, too, against the damning sins of later life, and holding out a horrid vision of the fate of those who gave themselves to vice and lust, and took their pleasure in fleshly dalliance.

And it was true, all true! She knew it, and inside she turned sick and fluid with fright. She threw her arms in front of her to guard against the apparitions that danced and yawed and shifted beyond her. She felt suddenly disembodied, lacking even the strength to stand up. Her legs were watery and loose and when she felt them give, she failed to catch herself, and went stumbling down.

She struck in a gasp of breath. The stones tore at her clothing and the hard caliche slammed its baking heat against the length of her body. From her throat a low cry came. She got her arms beneath her, and tried to rise; and then her eyes caught Ansel bending above her, his long face coming down to her, hard and cruel. It was Ansel, all right, but in another way, it wasn't Ansel.

"Keep away!" she cried out.

"What's the matter with you?"

"Keep away!" she cried out again. She tried again to rise, but nothing seemed to work right. The earth surged, and overhead the sky dipped, swaying. She felt herself going down, down, down. Was this death?

"Goddamn it, what's the matter with you?" Ansel said.

"Keep away from me!" she yelled at him, but he wouldn't keep away from her. He bent further;

and she could feel his hands upon her body, pulling her up. "Keep away! I hate you! I hate you!"

Still, he seized her arms, and pulled upon them and lifted her. His face came over hers, and she could see his hard eyes narrow and widen in the way of one who has possessed a thing and sees its loss threatened.

"No!" she cried, but he was bending above her now and forcing her back. She pounded on his thick chest with her fists, crying, "No! No! Devil! Devil!"

But she could not break his grip; and as though he *was* the devil, whose claims upon her were past denying any longer, he bent her backward and brought his mouth down onto her dried and cracked lips. She felt his fingers spreading across her shoulder blades; then beneath her bodice, she could feel his thumbs creep toward her breasts, searching and pressing. She felt him spread his body against her, felt it spread all over her; and when his tongue plied into her mouth to do what it liked to do there, she felt absorbed and drawn into him.

Against her will, and of their own accord, her arms came up and around him and her hands drew him close to her. It was nothing she could help doing, nor could she will against it in her mind. It was as if the very wantonness for which she suffered had joined against her with the ageless evil, of which Ansel was the living, black image, and she could fight him no longer.

Nor did she wish to fight him any longer; for she had moved across that borderland where hate and love bear each other's likeness, and where despair becomes ecstasy.

The pounding of the passion that he aroused within her was as the pounding of the fierce sun in the sky, and she was lost, lost, lost. . . .

When she regained consciousness Ansel was kneeling beside her, fanning her with his hat. Dazedly she said, "I had a dream, a nightmare."

Ansel muttered, "Well, you're all right now. Get up, damn it, we've got to move on."

Maggie shuddered. Had she merely dreamed this—was it a reënactment in her mind of what had happened between her and Ansel many times before . . . ?

7.

Otto Wagner had to laugh; or maybe a better word would be snort, as he didn't really feel much like laughing by now. But it was still good enough for a snort to look around behind him and see the girl coming out of a faint and that slick gambler fanning her, trying to get her on her feet, and none too gently, either.

But aside from that, there wasn't much to laugh at any more; or to snort at, whichever. Except that you might see a joke in how a fellow going against your grain can get you way out on the end of a limb you wouldn't have gotten onto by yourself.

Just now it wasn't so funny, when none of it would ever have happened if he hadn't let his tongue get so careless.

Of course, it wasn't all his fault. It was the doings of Lieutenant Patterson, too; for if he hadn't niggled over the water, Otto wouldn't have let himself appear so sure that he could take them to it. If Patterson had only backed off and let it go at "pretty sure," Otto knew he would be confident about it, still.

But, no; the Lieutenant wouldn't let him get away with that. He wouldn't leave it be at "pretty sure." Otto's being only pretty sure about the water wasn't good enough; he had to have it all laid out, as clear as he might see it in a regimental order; he had to worry it, like a dog might worry an old rag, before he turned loose of it.

And as soon as Otto had let himself be goaded to that wise remark about a fellow knowing the water holes, once he's seen them, and maybe drunk from them, why, he got scared.

Still and all, egged on or not, saying it was his own doing; and the blame for it would have to rest on his shoulders.

It was pride that made him say it—the oldest and most ornery of all the sins that mankind is plagued with.

What really scared him was what Patterson had said about a person's memory. Memory was a shifty business at any age, but it was trickiest when you got old.

It's easy enough to keep an image in your mind, with all the little details just the way you put them there for safekeeping. But just you come to face it in the flesh again, after a piece of time has gone by. Then you'll see how easy it can come unhitched from your remembrance. Everything has moved around and doesn't look the way it used to any more.

So Patterson was right about it, after all. Maybe the Lieutenant couldn't help that, being the kind who makes you rise up on your back legs, no matter what he might say.

Still and all, Otto couldn't bring himself to hold it too much against Lieutenant Patterson, especially when he thought about the part his *own* mouth had played. Moreover, as it set him down to quarrel with people, he leaned more to excusing Patterson than to faulting him.

For one thing, he looked pretty young; though not so young as Muller looked. But he was young enough and being military, too, he had to have things certain-sure, without any doubts fraying out from the edges.

Soldiers never liked to hear about a place that *might* be where you said it was; that scared them, and made them mad, too. They even worried about a place that you were absolutely sure of. The only thing they liked was having it on a map, something they could see and measure and pin down.

But mostly it was just that he was new to the job, and anxious that he account for himself the best way he could. Coming from St. Louis with him, Wagner had plenty of time to get his range, and you could tell, all right. You had only to see him sitting there as solemn as a barn owl with the weight of the nation on him, and how he rubbed his brass and gilt with his sleeves. They're a good deal like pretty girls, forever preening at them-selves.

Since his orders had him posted to the Presidio in San Francisco, it was likely that this change in plans was unsettling for him. No doubt, Otto thought, he'd be impatient, too, if he was on his own hook for the first time, and the situation wasn't covered by what he'd learned in school.

Even so, for all that he excused him for being new and young, Patterson was still a graveling kind of fellow. You take the way he carried on about the distance. Hardly had they walked for half an hour than he was going at Otto about it. In the desert air, even with the heat haze of summer, a thing will look closer than it really is.

Pretty near right off, he had his pants full of ants.

"How far to here, Wagner?" he started asking after a while.

"Oh, a little beyond a mile, maybe," Otto said. "Maybe a mile and a half. Little less, little more. We're getting along."

"It doesn't look it to me," he said. "Those hills don't look any nearer than they did at the coach."

"It's the air," Otto said. "It's different than what you're used to. Sometimes it fools a fellow."

Patterson was blond and tall, and had a way of looking at you that was almost like over-looking; that hump on his nose did it, maybe.

"Perhaps your distance is estimated wrong," he added.

"Not if it ain't changed any while I been gone. It's still the same as ever. Give or take a mile or two."

He was set to give or take those miles, no matter what.

For a while, then, they didn't speak much. The squabble had left them panting anyway, and going quiet was the best medicine. It never paid to hurry in the desert. You stretch your body moisture longer going slow and easy. Pretty much the same things goes for talking; the less you say, the more spit you save, and them as talk a lot are bound to get as dry as lime. The desert was never a place for gabbers.

With a crowd there was bound to be a few

folks bent to air their notions. And it wasn't in the Lieutenant to hold his tongue for long. It was easy to see that Otto's guessing at the distance was a kind of scandal to him, and he couldn't rest until he had that licked.

Maybe another mile went by and then he said, and smiling, too, so Otto would know the Army knew a few things, "Well, Wagner, we've come a mile since the last rest; a mile and two-tenths, to be exact."

The mere idea that he could give the miles as though he had a wheel to count the turns, was all that Otto needed.

"You got the proof?" he said right off.

"Oh, it's easy enough. I merely counted the steps I took since starting out. So many steps in a mile, you know."

"I'll agree on feet," Otto said. "You got to sell me on the steps, though. How do you know how far you go in a step?"

"Thirty inches; the regulation step. The inches are convertible to feet; and they, in turn, are convertible to miles. Everybody knows the feet in a mile. I merely interpolate the figures."

He laughed then, all of it coming through his long nose, and glanced at Otto. But Otto just scowled. It was the saying of such things that graveled him; that and using words that hardly sounded decent—and sighting along his nose.

Even more, he was scared again. No matter the

size and shape of the words that Patterson used, Otto had the sense of how he'd got his figures for the mileage, and it bothered him. The scare came at him fresh again to think he hadn't known that, too; or just as bad, maybe having known about it at an earlier time, and having forgotten it. Worse, now that he was started on such thoughts, was all the other chances of forgetting what he should remember.

As anyone who'd traveled in the desert knew, there was an awful lot about it to keep in mind; and on the other side of the same coin, an awful lot to forget. And now that this nose-peering schoolroom soldier boy had got his doubts stirred up, these things began to fly at him like bats from an old barn.

Take, for instance, snakes. He'd hardly thought of snakes when mining in the old days—and he had gone prowling into the snakiest kind of country—like over there along the Rio San Pedro—save to mark them well before stepping.

But he was thinking of them now; their ways, and whether or not he remembered right about them. One thing was their skins, when they shed them, and when they went blind. At that time, when they couldn't see around them, they were at their worst, and like to strike at anything that came in reach, without warning. Just to pass where he might feel you in the ground will set a diamondback snapping. But was it summer or winter that they shed their skins and went blind? Or was it both?

Just to wonder was enough to make him shiver and walk along walleyed, looking out for them. Not that he was scared, especially, but that was when he knew what he might expect of them. Now he didn't. Then there were the stones— another thing to plague him; something else that had slipped away from his memory.

The group were resting under a flimsy patch of greasewood, hardly any shade at all when you considered it. None of them had very much to say by that time. Jager and his girl friend sat off alone, the girl having her head down on her raised knees, and Jager apart from her by a couple of yards.

But the gambler seemed a queer kind anyway; he still wore his coat. The Lieutenant had his coat on, too, or tunic, what he called it, but that was different; you would expect that.

Muller was on his back, an arm thrown over his face, and Otto would have bet his head was pounding like a medicine drum. Beside him, Huston had an elbow propped beneath himself, and he was watching Muller in a way that made you think the boy had some meaning to him.

Then Otto noticed Huston picking something from the sand and putting it in his mouth. At first he only marked it in his thoughts. But when Muller did the same thing, it got to fretting Otto's mind, so before he thought, he asked what it was.

"They're stones," Muller said, taking his arm down to look at Otto. "What'd you think, Pop?"

"To induce the flow of saliva," Huston put in. "Some comfort in it, if nothing else."

Then he looked at Otto in an odd way, a searching kind of look; and in a moment Otto had the sense of what it might mean. It was like he had been judged and found wanting somehow. It was like he'd been unmasked for something other than he'd made himself out. And it didn't help to know that he'd recalled about the stones.

All at once, he couldn't meet Huston's eyes. They seemed to ask too much he couldn't answer. They were kind enough, and gentle; but still they asked him why *he* hadn't known about the stones, too. If he hadn't known about so simple a thing, or had forgot—they seemed to ask as clear as any voice—how could he know where the water was? Or *if* it was?

Otto looked away, feeling Huston's and now Muller's eyes on him, and feeling a queer shaking seize him.

He watched his hand, seeing the blue veins stand out in the warm flesh, the glisten of sweat on it, like varnish.

The hand was old, he thought—the brown hairs gray, the skin grained, a knuckle bulging from an old break. The finger bone beneath the bulge of cartilage was old, and the long bone connecting with the wrist, and beyond, the arm.

They all were old, he thought; every bone in his body—his head, too, and suchever brain as was inside of it. Just now, that seemed the oldest thing of all.

He felt Huston still looking at him; and Muller, too, sort of leering. In the way that thoughts can pass unspoken through the heads of many, all were more alert now, while they looked from Otto to the mountain, and back, as if each had come to know the meaning of those stones.

At last he dared to look at it, too. It was nearer by a good deal now than earlier. They were pretty close to halfway, maybe a shade beyond; anyway, they had come close enough for him to think he might be able to see the part that held the tanks; maybe even a little green of trees standing over the water.

He couldn't, though; he didn't see any trees, nor did any part of it jog his memory. All he saw was stone and light and the shaking watery motion which the heat made of everything. He stared until his eyeballs seemed to crack in the hot air, but still he couldn't see the tanks, nor anything else that looked as it should.

He knew the mountains were the Tortolitas; he was sure enough about that; but having said that, he had said everything. It was enough to make him wonder if the water that he'd drunk in the past wasn't in some other range of mountains, somewhere far off from those ahead.

8.

It was after they'd got started again that Otto began to notice the heat more. It seemed to be an inner, gnawing, animal kind of heat that ate and sucked his body moisture. It kept pouring up from somewhere deep down and spreading out inside of him; radiating through him, so that he seemed to glow in the way of iron that is being blown in the forge.

Sometimes it seemed to give a shimmer to what he looked at—but a shimmer different from what was given them by the trembling of the air; a shimmer inside his eyes. And other times it made the different parts of his body seem strangers to each other; so that a step his brain had told his foot to make might not be made so quickly as it should be made, and he'd stumble. This heat was heavy, too, and had a swarming weight that made it seem that he bore the whole load of a burning roof on his shoulders and head.

Maybe it had started with Muller and Huston watching him as they had. Maybe it was there before, growing in him all the while, needing only Muller's and Huston's knowing, searching look at him to bring it out.

It might have been that his belief in doing what he thought he could do had held it back earlier.

But that was all changed now; having been unmasked had fixed that. A man can stand a lot of damage so long as he is sure in his mind about whatever it is he's after. Just let him feel a doubt about it, then you'll see how quick it changes. No sooner does his faith get shook up than all he's gone through comes back to kick at him.

That was how it was with the mountain now. He couldn't think how many times he'd cast up his memory of those hills, and every time they'd overlaid upon the ones that stuck up out of the ground ahead.

Now that he had lost his faith, and had this wild heat eating him away, and changing everything, they seemed more and more like hills that he had never before seen anywhere.

Still, he wasn't the only one to show the heat by this time. All of them were running down like clocks that should be wound before it was too late.

Walking was torture now. It wasn't only the burning of the feet, but the weight and size they'd took on. They made a load that sometimes had you leaning forward to get started. His legs were stiffer, too, and more awkward, the knees not bending right, so that a person often looked as if he had a load in his trousers. Even the girl looked it, though it was hard to tell what kind of trousers *she* wore, if any.

In resting, they were getting so they only cared

to flop and blow until they moved on. Long back, as he recalled, they might try to find a clean place to rest, so that their clothing didn't get too dirty. Now, nobody cared. All of them were soaked, the sweat marks rimmed around with rings of salt, and often, where the sweat had touched the ground, there'd be a skim of mud.

Along about that time, when they were getting not to care about their clothes, Muller took to fuming at Otto. He'd been as touchy as a sore boil right along, and now he started calling out to Otto, asking where the water was.

Maybe he'd start by saying, "Hey, grandpa, where you keepin' that water anyway?"

Then Otto might call over his shoulder, "Just ahead, here, sonny."

Then Muller might say, "Where? Where? Show me where."

So Otto would tell him, "Not far now. Only a ways beyond. You'll see soon enough."

Then Muller might give out a braying kind of laugh, and say, "That's a good one. Don't you wish you'd had that slug of muleshoe now?"

And Otto would then answer, "No, I sure don't; and I bet you wish you'd quit before you did."

Saying that told Otto that he'd hit a sore point with Muller; something that he maybe knew was so, but wouldn't even admit it to himself. Just to hear it though would rile him.

"You're lyin' about the water!" he shouted at

Otto. "I don't think you got any idea where it is! I don't even believe there's any out here. It's all a story, one of your silly tales!"

In between the times he badgered Otto, he might ride off in other directions. He let Lieutenant Patterson know he had a poor opinion of the Army; which sounded like he might be drawing on experience.

A couple of times the Lieutenant turned around and glared, like he was speculating on that himself, or wondering how it might fit in with the feeling of bad blood that lay between them. There was more than just rubbing tempers there.

Muller had some words about a girl in California, too; someone he was on his way to see, it sounded like. They weren't such good words though.

He was troubled by a lot of things, but hardly any of it came out clear. Hearing him, you'd think it all frothed over with the heat of the day, or with that muleshoe that he'd had earlier. Not that he'd had an awful lot; but even a little can make a difference on a boiling summer day when you're set afoot, unexpected. It scalds you out, and frazzles your brains, too.

The things he said had Otto's back up more than once; but more than being riled, Otto was inclined to pity him. From keeping a kind of secret quiet in the coach, he'd all at once turned out to be needling and quarrelsome. Not only that, but he seemed to know a good deal more about the country than he'd first let on. Apart from the heat and what he'd drunk, he seemed driven by some other thing that had lain quiet inside of him until the coach was wrecked and they were all of them turned loose upon the desert on foot.

At least he didn't have to listen to it all, like Huston did. Not that Huston seemed to mind; he just went along with Muller there, as if he was on guard against his stumbling or falling.

Now that Otto thought of it, Huston seemed to be another odd one. Odd in another way than anyone else. It was as if he wasn't given to the same concerns that bothered others—he hardly ever squabbled; for a fact, he stopped them. By now he was as wobbly as any other, but it didn't touch him in the same way—not inside anyway. His face was still calm, and seemed to hold a kind of sad peace in it. Somehow it seemed to give the notion that nothing mattered too much.

It must have been around four o'clock when Lieutenant Patterson noticed the change in the cloud over the Catalinas, off to the south. The sunlight now struck Otto under his hat with full force on the left side of his face; and a cloud beginning at noon above the mountains rarely came to anything until the afternoon was well on. The shadows were on his right, too.

"I declare," Patterson said, on first noting it,

"that cloud is quite a bit bigger now. Darker, too."

"They allus get like that around now," Otto said. "It's the way they are."

"It seems to be nearing us a little," Patterson said. "See how the top is reaching out."

"That's another thing they allus do," Otto said. "They get that anvil look about them, up on top. It don't need to mean anything particular."

"Why," said Patterson, "it certainly looks to me as if it was coming closer."

"It's account they flatten out like that, that's all," Otto said. "Then they got nowhere else to go, save sideways."

He was now aware of having a feeling about that cloud; or, more, about this talk of it—though it was hard to place just yet. Out in this draining heat, a man's mind was slow to move to new thoughts.

"If that's the case, is there any reason why it shouldn't reach this far?"

"Maybe the top will," Otto said. "But that ain't where the rain is, if it's got any rain."

"Why not?" Patterson said.

"Too white. The rain's in the dark part, down lower. It's the winds moving around, going up and down, that make it spread."

"Well, then, if it keeps on spreading, is there any reason why it can't reach us eventually?"

"It ain't impossible," Otto said. "I just ain't countin' on it, that's all. Mostly such rains, them as form on the mountains in the summer, down here anyway, stay close. I don't say they *allus* do; just mostly. That being the case, we ain't likely to get it, account we're pretty well north."

"Well, we can do no harm by praying that this is one of the exceptions," the Lieutenant said.

Otto knew now what bothered him about that cloud. If he got to thinking that it might come north, or hoping anyway, it would mean that he was looking somewhere else beside the tanks for their water. It would mean that he mightn't believe in them any more. It would be the same thing as admitting that he'd forgotten where they really were, just as he'd forgotten about those stones, and about the ways of snakes, and it would mean that he had no more faith in himself at all. It might even mean, like Muller said, that he was only telling himself a tale.

"Go ahead and pray," Otto said. "Ain't none but Indians believe in it though."

Then he knew he'd put more strength behind it than he'd meant to, because Lieutenant Patterson looked oddly at him for a moment before he turned his head again toward the cloud. It was almost, Otto thought, as if he had told Patterson that he hoped it wouldn't rain.

9.

Well, the hills were there anyway; Wagner could be sure of that much. However they might change and shift in the trembling air, being steep and ragged one time, and squat and more strung out the next, they still remained there.

For all the fact that walking now was like a treadmill must be, they seemed nearer than before.

It would be nice to know how far they really were, he thought. And it would be nice, too, to know how far they'd really walked across this plain. All they'd had to go on was those figures of Lieutenant Patterson's.

Patterson wasn't giving the figures now. He didn't seem to care to check upon the distance any more, nor did he move out with his regulation step any longer—noting the feet and inches and the miles, so that he might interpolate—or whatever it was. Nowatimes he was more taken with the cloud, and he watched it all the time, as if that helped to coax it nearer to them.

He wasn't wearing his tunic now, either. Otto couldn't remember when that happened, but he remembered how. All at once, while they were walking, Patterson's hands began to work the buttons loose. He did it like he had a pain of some kind, and all the while his fingers wrenched and pulled, he wouldn't look. His eyes remained ahead, as though they couldn't bear to see such disgrace. Otto was pleased to see him unbend a little. He even got a laugh out, and Patterson shot him a glance that said he'd heard.

Then, only a little ways beyond where he had thrown his tunic over his shoulder, Patterson took his penknife out and slashed the insteps of his boots. And then, as if to go whole hog, he ran the blade around them at the ankle, then ripped them up the back, took the leg parts off and threw them away.

Otto didn't laugh that time though; it was different than the tunic. Taking off the tunic was meant to ease his back, but cutting off his boots was a matter of going on. Otto didn't like to watch him, either; it was too much like retreating in a battle, or passing out the last of his ammunition to the troops.

Time was getting so queer by now that it was hard to tell for sure when all that happened, but it had. The Lieutenant now shuffled along with his trousers flapping at his ankles, his fine pretty boots cut down to nothing but the soles.

Time was getting queer in another way. A whole long line of things and places that had nothing to do with where he now was marched in his head. They were as real as life, though he had lived them long before this time.

Of a sudden, he was thinking of the Mississippi River. It seemed to come from nowhere, and he saw the muddy waters and the high trees that arched above them. Standing on a wharf that jutted outward on its dark pilings, there were bales of white cotton, and beyond it on the river, eddies widened where a catfish wallowed. Back some from the old wharf, a bearded man was sitting on the gallery of a shabby wooden building, lounging with his feet on the shaky railing. And it was him.

Then he went away from there—over the plains and mountains to an altogether different country, where the air was lighter, and where the rivers went madly through their narrow beds, and came streaming cold and clear from peaks and ranges that might bear snow on them for all of time. There was timber, too, some so big that even seeing it was doubting it. Far off in the west, across the valleys and the smaller coastal ranges, the wide-breasted sea curved outward toward the world's rim.

That time, when he saw himself, he was a younger man. He was some straighter, too, and flat-muscled, and his beard was black and glossy in the sunlight that fell upon him at the river's edge. He was leaning on a rocker box which other men were filling with sand and gravel, where water ran to wash it free of gold dust. Up the bank a ways, smoke came out of a pipe in the roof of a tent; and from the timber nearby, a Chinaman came walking in his shuffling way, his arms filled with kindling, his queue jiggling.

There were soda lakes, and beds of white gypsum, wide flats of alkali, and playas deep in yellow dust that choked and suffocated. There were deep arroyos, and canyons where the sun might not touch bottom save an hour in a day. There were mirages—where cities rose and fell, where sailing vessels spread canvas, and locomotives pulled their trains of ghostly cars away to nowhere at all.

Sometimes there'd be a flowing creek, notching through the empty hills and plains; but often as not, it would only be sand shaped to the contour of a bed that would be lying empty against the summer rains, or run-off from the melt of winter snows.

There was a sound of picks and shovels digging, and of burros hawing. The men were always bent above their pans or their rockers, seeking, searching.

Once a girl was there. She was back beside the Mississippi in a much younger time. It was long ago, oh, long, long ago; so far back that he'd had no beard of any kind in that day. She was dressed in homespun of her own making, and in the honest way that it was plain, she, too, was plain; but her eyes were shining at him so that he took no notice of the plainness. They spoke to him, saying in their warm way that he had only to say the word himself.

He hadn't though. Maybe the breeze had carried him a scent; maybe a river boat had picked that moment to hoot, and so distracted him; but whichever, it had been enough to draw him away. And rather than say the one word that would have changed his whole life he had gone digging someplace. It didn't matter that he'd had before him that which makes most men happy to find. He had all the same gone off seeking and searching, for he knew not what, elsewhere.

He knew what caused it now, this having time catch up with him and mix with what was happening to him out on this flat. It was what a man's mind began to do when he was drowning.

It was the first he'd really thought of dying out in this place. Maybe he should be scared, and he knew he would have been scared before, if he had faced it, except that there was too much else for him to be afraid of to let that in, too. As for being scared now that it was very possible and real, maybe he had got too tired and worn down to be scared. Anyway he wasn't.

Thinking of it only made him sad, because his life had been wasted. Never in all of his years of poking through the hills and deserts had he found that great bonanza. Nor had he in that long time come on that other something, either: and there had been something else—nameless, and so vague in his mind that he'd have to stumble onto it in order to recognize it. But he wouldn't now, any more; the chance for that was gone, too, just like it was for any gold.

Now, too, all at once, he knew he wouldn't find the water, for he lacked the strength to keep on going. That, in some way, seemed to be the worst of all. Knowing that about himself told him that he was a failure altogether. It was bad enough a man should go out knowing he was useless to himself; but failing those who had depended on him, too, made it seem better that he never had lived.

All at once Otto stumbled. He began to fall, but the Lieutenant caught his arm and bore him back up. As he stood there swaying, trying to make his feet work, Muller's voice came at him from somewhere behind.

"What's the matter, grandpa, you quittin' on us?"

Otto turned his head and looked for Muller in the shimmering blindness of his sight. He tried to speak, but not much came out beyond a croaking whistle.

"By God, it surely looks like you are," Muller said.

Otto turned his head again and looked back. Patterson was trying to start him forward once more, but he was drawn to look back at Muller. He was trying to think why he had felt any pity for the younger man.

"I guess you finally saw the truth of all them lies you been telling us," Muller called out.

This time Patterson turned and looked at Muller, too.

"Leave him alone, confound it. He's doing the best he can."

"Doing the best he can to get us lost," Muller said. "He's got us out in the middle of nowhere, and now he quits."

Otto tried again to speak, but as before, only a scraping sound came out of his throat.

"Goddamn it, Muller!" Patterson said in a shout. "Leave him alone!"

"I guess I got a right to ask him if he's quittin'!" Muller shouted back.

"You got no right to make it worse than it is!" the Lieutenant shouted.

"I've got every right in the world to know why he took us out here, then lay down on us!" Miller shouted. "Don't tell me about my rights!"

The Lieutenant pulled again on Otto's arm, trying to start him moving forward. Muller's voice was like a chant in Otto's ears, a chant of all his failures; and was enough to make him seek his feet and make another effort to drive them forward in the right way. He watched them in the blur and shimmer, seeing them as belonging to another person, and speaking to them in his mind, urging and coaxing them.

Walk, walk, stumble, shuffle, his mind said to

his feet and legs and whole body. Get that leg up, get it forward, get that foot down. There. Now, bring that other leg up, get it up there—whup!—no further. Hah. Now, do it again; do it again and still again. Keep on moving, feet; keep on going. Don't you dare to stop again; should you quit again, we won't get there, and we got to get there. We got to get there, hear? We got to show that young loudmouth we can find the water. So don't you quit again.

The feet shuffled, the body pitched and swayed, the knees flexed, and the legs reached out their meager distance. The head inclined upon the red neck, the vague eyes held upon the nearest foreground, the scalded shoulders rounded to the arching of the spine, the arms swung loose, like lengths of rope, the hands slack and fingers curled.

Walk, stumble, shuffle, drag it; drag it, Otto, drag it, Wagner, you old bastard. You got to get there, Otto; you got to get *them* there. You got to show them you can do it; you got anything left in you, you got to show it now.

Now a voice came into Otto's mind; the same as when Muller had taunted him. It even sounded something like Muller.

Ho, there, crazy man, said the voice, how you talk. Get who where?

Get these people there, that's who.

Get them where, old man? Where you think you're going to get them?

Get them to the water, that's where. To the water.

Water? Ho, you dreamer! Who said there was water out here?

Nobody said so. Nobody had to say so, account I seen it. I drunk it, too, seein' you're so nosy.

Sand, Otto, sand. That's all you'll find out here.

That's a lie! A no-good, scheming lie! Just you wait and see. There's water in the tanks!

Tanks? I don't know of any tanks. What tanks are those? A notion, that's all. You're getting loony in your old age.

That ain't so! I'm as good as ever!

Oh, Otto, how you talk. You never should have left your boarding house, that's what. You got no business coming back out here again. Not when you're as old as you are. You ought to be in your rocker, watching the river boats go by.

That ain't so, neither! I'm as fit as ever I was. I got the same right to be out here as in the old days!

Pshaw, Otto, so you say. Where at is the water, then?

In the tanks, goddamn it, like I said. In the tanks!

So? But where at are the tanks?

In the hills, that's where, goddamn it! In the hills!

Oh, Otto, how you do take on. Where at are the hills?

• • •

It was then the weight bore down upon him in a mass too great for him to carry any longer. An iron bar that had been raised to white heat had formed behind his eyes. The sun made such a heavy pounding in his head that his body seemed to shake and vibrate with it while queer lights went on and off, glowing and fading. His feet were going all ways now, denying any say-so over them at all, while the burden of the sun, the sky and all he knew about himself, pushed and crushed at him. Even the things that Muller'd yelled at him, things he'd known and Muller had put to voice, couldn't force him onward any further. They had served to drive him for a ways, though how far he couldn't tell, but they worked no longer. Nothing worked any more—he was finished.

All at once a knee gave under him, then the other buckled. He could feel himself beginning to go, and Patterson this time could not stop him; the earth beneath him oozed and changed, but there was no help for it. Looking down, he saw it tilt and sway, and saw the small stones grow larger as he neared them.

One knee struck, and when the other struck, his hands went out to shield his face. For a space, when there was only white emptiness inside his head, the hard jar numbed his wits; but in another moment the edges of the sharp stones had needled through him a pain that cleared his head like cold water. He made some kind of sound inside his throat, and put his head up while his eyes closed down against the shiver of hurt.

When he opened them he saw the trees ahead of them.

"The trees," he said.

"What?" Patterson said. He was standing over Otto, trying to pull him up. Muller and Huston had come up by then, too.

"The trees," Otto said again, and they were still there.

"Where?" Huston said. "What trees?"

"Beneath the mountain," Otto said. "Up on that little knoll."

It was so, and he could see them well now. A flush of green cropped out upon a small stony hill beneath the steep flank of the mountain, and now he knew they were the mesquite trees. All of the memories and images and doubts that had been whirling in his head took one last turn around, and locked in place.

"Look at them," he said.

He was getting up now, slowly though, so he could hold the trees in his sight. He was fearful that they'd go away, and that he'd lose them, if he hurried or stopped looking at them.

"Look at them!" he said. He was standing and the trees were still there. "Look! Look!" Then he laughed. "Oh, look at them! See the trees! The mesquite trees! The tanks are in the trees!"

He laughed again; he made little dancing steps and shouted while he watched them on their stony outcrop. "Oh, the trees, see the trees! The water is in the trees!" He pointed at them while he hopped and danced and laughed; he felt young and springy, full of beans and vinegar, like he'd been newly born.

They were staring at the trees, the others, only then beginning to believe and understand, when he broke loose of them. He started running. The trees were up the knoll, a couple of hundred yards off. He could see them very clearly now; still he didn't dare to take his eyes from them, even while he ran toward them.

He ran, the way of his running a stumbling and a weaving, a tottering and a staggering from side to side, lunging and jolt-legged. But it didn't seem that way. It seemed to Otto that he ran on air, or that he skimmed and floated over the rough ground.

Sometimes he stumbled blindly into stands of greasewood; sometimes into catclaw or fishhook that ripped and shredded; but he held to a straight line toward the trees, never taking his eyes away from where they stood up green and waiting. There were gullies and draws that he staggered and wallowed through; rock, now, too, many rocks, and big, for he had come upon the outwash slope that spread out under the mountains. Sometimes he was able to see these stones in time to swerve around them; but more often, as he wasn't looking where his feet fell, they would bang his brogan or leg.

Still he ran on, tripping, falling, pushing up again and stumbling on—not feeling the jolts or the pains. His hands and knees were wet and bloody from falling, but he didn't feel the cuts and bruises any more than the jolts of falling. Nor did he feel that bar of heat behind his eyes now, nor even the weary burden that had dogged him for so long. None of that made any difference any more. He felt young and filled with fierce happiness. He felt himself right with the world; he felt dependable and useful, because he'd brought them in to water.

The feeling stayed with him until he reached the bottom of the stone outcrop. Then he entered a space of clear sand, and drew up to a swaying halt. Something in the sand had caught his eyes, but when he stopped, the beating of his heart was so heavy that he could only stare at first, while what he saw kept coming and going.

Then things steadied down, and he could make out the marks, prints made by the hoofs of horses; and of riders, too, who had dismounted in this place to lead the horses up the slope.

There were three, from what he made out, and when he'd looked enough to understand, he felt sad again. It wasn't the same as he had felt before, though; more the way you feel when you have done a great thing, and see it all gone for nothing. There was nothing he could see up there, not even the flick of a tail among the overhanging trees; but they were there, because the tracks were freshly laid down.

It made him want to weep; and the oldness that he now felt was like none that he had known while coming over the desert. Still, a part of the gladness and the triumph that he'd known there for a moment went on living in the sadness. At least he had proved up on what he'd said. It almost seemed that he had justified his life, and that nothing that might now happen could spoil it. He'd broken even anyway, all things considered. He'd proved that it wasn't all a waste. Maybe they'd never get to taste the water, but he'd brought them to it.

Behind him came a sound, and then the others were pushing through the greasewood into the open. He turned, seeing them burned and ragged, leaning on each other like battle-wounded. It was Muller who let out the squall, sounding half wild.

"What's the matter? Ain't it up there, like you been sayin'?"

Otto couldn't make himself speak right away. It was queer and strange, somehow like it might be had he been a god who'd had a look at things to come, and wished to spare his worshippers the pain of what lay ahead. They all looked so relieved and hopeful, and now he had to kill it off. He even regretted a little telling Muller—he might never have got so far except that Muller ragged him. It was easy to be forgiving now.

"Well?" and it was Patterson now; he drew up to Otto and stopped. "Is it there, or isn't it?"

"Yes," Otto said at last. "Yes, it's there, all right. This is the place."

And then he told them that Indians had reached the water ahead of them.

10.

The Lieutenant said, "Ah, well, ah, well"; and letting it go with that, he grew quiet. With his eyes closed, he leaned his head against the island of high rock which rose behind them on the ground, where they were sitting.

"Fine," Muller said, "this is fine. This is great."

"Ah, quit your yelling," Jager told him. "You got here, didn't you?"

"So what?" Muller said. "I could be well along the way to Picacho now, too. But, no, I let you talk me into this!"

"Go easy, son," Huston said to Muller. "You'll only waste your strength, and nothing is accomplished that way."

"A fat lot of good it's going to do me here," Muller said, and then he turned on Wagner with a vile word, as though he felt the Indians to be Wagner's planned doing.

Wagner had no answer, however. He was lying on his stomach in the shade thrown down upon them from the rock, his elbow under his face, sleeping. And he deserved to sleep, Huston thought.

Miss Hale was quiet, too. She was crying now though, and he could see her shoulders move, and how the sharp emotion pulled at her features. Still, there were no tears; and though he knew that tears might be a luxury that her body could ill afford by this time, the sight was strange, even so.

And it was a shame, too, he thought; for he had liked her rather inviting beauty of earlier in the day. But now that they had come to this, the agony of tearless weeping brought her near ugliness.

Huston sat on the ground against the warm rock. The rock covered a fair-sized piece of ground—half an acre maybe, or more—out beyond the outcrop or low hill. The surface was cracked and seamed by every cycle of weather, and the fractures in the rotten granite were choked with Spanish bayonet and prickly pear and salt bush.

It was high enough so that the sun, now well down, threw out an apron of dark shade around the base where they were sitting or lying down.

Of course, the rock still held in it a measure of

the day's heat, and it was hard to say if the weather was really much cooler there yet. But sun and shade were minor qualities, just now anyway, in view of what they knew about the water.

Well, Huston thought, it was a shame that it should come to this. It was bad enough for these people, who now lay on the earth like rag dolls who had been thrown down at random; or as if the impact of their knowledge of the Indians had felled them where they had been standing.

Yet, it was an interesting thing, too. That would be the clinical view—and for a moment he was able to see it that way. Over his years of medical practice he had often marveled at what the human body could withstand while hope remained alive. Moreover, there seemed to be a connection between the nature of the goal in view, or of the hope, and the body's tolerance of stress in order to achieve the goal, or to realize the hope. Providing hope did not die out, the body could endure a great deal of suffering.

Well, he had seen it work that way; and then again, he had seen it work the other way around. So that, when the goal was lost, or when the hope of it collapsed, the endurance of the body was apt to follow soon after.

That was interesting, too, and more than once in past years he'd felt the subject to hold promise for some kind of paper for a medical journal. Of course, that had been quite a while ago, when he was younger and had possessed the drives and urges that a younger man has. Now, though, it had been quite a long time since writing medical articles had been interesting to consider; or since much of anything had been of interest.

All the same, he could not help but think that the reaction of these people to finding Indians at the water would have furnished ample source material for a work of that kind.

They were quiet now; for some time they had been lying or sitting, silent on the heated ground. They avoided looking at the trees, as if the sight of them, so near with what they promised yet withheld from them, could not yet be borne; and instead, let their eyes go toward the Catalinas where the darkened, swelling cloud might offer new hope.

Watching his companions, Huston knew he felt compassion for them all, especially for the younger ones, for they always seemed to find the specter of defeat a reflection on their personal selves.

He tried to think when he had felt the same way—and it was some time; for a long while now, he had believed that one's middle years brought him to an awareness of certain truths. However it might reach him, through the slow erosion of the years, or through some series of incidents—he would come, in time, to see the true face of things. After that, he could see that nothing really mattered much. What they'd found here had not surprised him very much, for he had felt the venture to be futile from the beginning. And he had felt no more surprise that Indians held the water than that they'd found the water in the first place.

Nor was he especially surprised that he should feel no anxiety for the danger of their new predicament. If he felt anything at all, it was something of the same acceptance that he'd felt toward all that life had brought him in the past ten years. Some time or other, death was bound to come; and by and large, its manner was a detail. For him, at least, the difference that he saw between thirst and Indians was small. Death would mean the end of all this pointless wandering, of endless self-indictment, of somber, black memory. There would be peace where there had been no peace in ten years, and sorrow would be no more with him.

It was queer how the thought took hold of him, how welcome it seemed. He could feel it building in his mind as though it were some new and dangerous toy that has been forbidden to a child and is therefore more fascinating.

Huston let his glance move up the knoll. The rise went up a hundred yards or more, until it ended in the clutter of rock beneath the green trees. In between, the ground was rough with smaller stones, but it was bare of any useful cover. Well, there was a scatter of prickly pear and ocotillo. But they were spindly things that offered small protection and were useless anyway because they stood too near the outwash. Beyond them there would be no shelter for someone trying to make the long climb. The Indians would have him nailed down before he made it more than halfway, if not sooner.

Looking at the long slope, he felt the sinister suggestion that was carried to him as the shaking heat waves rose upward. The thought repelled him, but it also beckoned to him. Perhaps even, he was more attracted than warned away.

It would be so simple. He had only to rise from where he sat, go out into open ground and begin to climb; climbing slow and steady, being careful not to stumble, so that he would make a good target. At almost any time he might expect an arrow. He would watch for it and keep his eyes upon that slot up there. Most likely it would come from there, and now he wondered what it would be like. Would he see it coming at him—the warhead and the long cane shaft and bright, clean feathers? Or would there be a single beam of sunlight to denote its motion, seen all in a single glance together with the impact of its growing out of him?

On the other hand, they might not kill him right away, but let him come to a better range, so that the arrow might have force enough to pass entirely through his body. At least, in that event, he would be spared the need to look upon it in that second of oblivion; and perhaps it would be more tidy, too.

Then again, it might not happen that way, either. Rather than strike him down while he was climbing, they might let him come up all the way; and that he knew would frighten him, for little could be worse than what he knew would then follow.

Then would come the cutting and the skinning, and all the other things for which they had such genius—the hollow, wavery screaming, and the mess of blood and entrails while the brains oozed down among the flames and ashes of the fire they would set under his skull.

But this would be an end, even so. And while it would mean pain beyond any in his experience, so also would it mean atonement. And death would be relatively quick. He could hardly last beyond an hour or two in his present state—a little more, perhaps. Surely it would go more quickly than Charley and Louise had gone when they had been consumed by typhus—if it had been typhus.

Now in the eye of his mind, the dusky room appeared, the dim shuttered windows. It came readily to his sight, for it was never far, though close to twelve years had gone by. A faint light from the Chicago sky came through the shutter vanes.

They were lying in their beds quietly, the two beds drawn close together and the white sheets the only things clearly visible in the close, dismal room. He saw two waxen faces—that of the young boy and of the mother and wife—radiant with fever. Their eyes were wide and glassy with this heat, and all about the room there were the odors of creeping death.

He always saw them lying in that way, waiting while the smell of death grew stronger in their catchy, shallow breathing. He saw himself, too—desperate in that knowledge—seeking witlessly through what he'd learned about his own craft, and finding in the end that he hadn't learned enough about it.

That memory never changed; it was engraved and etched in his mind. It remained the same from day to day and year to year, as faithful as the round of seasons. However, he thought now, going up the hill would change it, and he could think about that.

But it was easy to see that no one else shared his feelings, at least not yet. They'd been quiet for a long time, resting from the draining weariness while they watched the far cloud swell and blacken; but now Lieutenant Patterson turned his head and studied the slope. After a moment of that he looked at Huston.

"Have you seen them yet?" he said.

"No, not yet. I've been watching, though."

The Lieutenant removed his cap and ran his hand over his head. His blond hair was dark with sweat and matted down with salt and the pressure of his cap. His ears were burned raw, and there were red slits along his caked lips.

"I wonder if they're really up there," he said.

"The old man said so," Huston said.

"We haven't seen them. How do we know? If there's been no rain out here, or wind, those tracks could be old."

"Maybe," Huston said, "but I incline to agree with him. He got us here; he was right about that much."

Patterson was quiet for a time, while his fingers idled with the cap. His gaze passed over the wide slope, and Huston wondered if Tacitus or Clausewitz had had anything to say to him about the taking of such positions. They'd still be read these days, he thought, even though the very live examples of the late rebellion were now available.

"Still, we can't be sure," Patterson said, "and we've got to find out. Unless we get rain here."

That brought Muller into it. Now that he was rested, he was calmer, but his feelings toward Patterson hadn't changed.

"Whyn't you go up there and see for yourself, if you don't believe him?"

"Poor tactics, if they are there," Patterson answered.

"Not if finding out is all that matters," Muller said, and he laughed. "You'll find out soon enough."

By ignoring him and turning back to Huston, Patterson made it plain that he would rather not become involved with Muller.

"Maybe I'll have a look around the bottom of this thing. I may be able to learn something more definite."

"Now there's a choice thought," Muller put in, meaning to be heard regardless. "I'd look 'em over good if I was you. Stare 'em down—that's the way to do it."

However he might wish to, Patterson could not ignore that.

"Generally speaking, Muller, it is always sound policy to reconnoiter the enemy's disposition." Patterson's eyebrows went up. "I don't wonder that you fail to understand, however."

"Yah?" Muller said, and then he laughed again. "Well, you go right ahead; reconnoiter 'em all you got. Maybe you can reconnoiter 'em clear to hell out of there."

Patterson managed to let it ride that time. He turned away from Muller, and pushing himself to his feet, started moving off. Huston watched him leaving in the ruins of his uniform, aware of feeling sorry for him in many ways. Muller made an effort to spit, but no spit came forth.

Except for Muller and Huston, no one else appeared to notice Patterson's leaving them. The girl had stopped her crying by now, and she was sitting with her eyes fixed on the swollen chambers of storm cloud. Jager, sitting near by, stared off in the same direction, but in a way that made you think he did not really see the cloud. It was hard to tell just what he might see, if anything, and it came to Huston that he had the knack of setting himself apart from things around him. You might think, to see him gazing out in that manner, that he had no care for what had happened to them, or for what might still happen to them. On the other hand, perhaps he did care; it was easy to be wrong about a person.

All the same, Jager bothered Huston. He would be a man who lived alone, a man who cultivated lonely habits; and you could never tell too much about such people on short acquaintance. Their circle of concern was small and nearly always self-centered. Jager's treatment of Miss Hale would be a good indication.

"Yah, him," Muller said in a while. He was standing now, puffing while he leaned against the rock and looked along the slope, where Patterson had gone. "He knows so much. Reconnoiter, hell."

Huston touched him, aware again that he saw something special in Muller.

"Easy does it," Huston said. "That doesn't do any good."

Muller turned his head and looked down at Huston. "Don't it?" he said. "You're great for sayin' that, seems to me. Fry up better goin' easy, do we? Just sit and take it, huh?"

"Well, that's so," Huston said, while he wondered what Muller saw in him. Then he added, "But I wasn't thinking of it that way."

"No? How was you then?"

"I was thinking," Huston began and paused, and after the pause went on slowly, "that you might give yourself away to him."

Then he stopped, and now he wondered whether he should talk in that way to Muller. Muller wasn't his responsibility, and Muller had made it plain enough that he resented help, or any interest in himself. Yet in Huston's mind, the resemblance that he saw was too strong for him to be indifferent. And even had it not been, there still remained young Muller's nearness of an age with Charley, had Charley been living now.

For a moment Muller said nothing, but only watched Huston. Then he said, "I guess I made some noise, not that much though."

"Enough for me to add things together," Huston said. "I walked with you, remember, coming over here."

Muller slid along the rock until he was sitting again; then he poked his finger into the sand and lowered his eyes. His clothes were oversized, Huston saw again, meant for a larger man. Likely he had bought them on the run, or had traded for them with his uniform while leaving Mesilla Valley. Coming down to it, he might have stolen them, though Huston shied away from that thought.

"All right," Muller said, glancing up, "now you know. So what?" His voice was wary, but defiant, too, like his eyes; as if whatever fear he had of Huston's turning him in to Patterson was overridden by his sense of frustration and failure. His plans had gone so badly wrong that he felt outraged by everything.

"Nothing," Huston said. "Nothing to me, that is," although he knew by now that wasn't exactly so. "It might mean something to Patterson, though."

"Yah?" Muller said, and with an effort pulled himself again to his feet, and looked along the bottom of the slope. But Patterson was now gone from sight around the curving shoulder of the rock. "It likely would, at that; just about his speed."

"I only said it might," Huston said.

"Still his speed. Big brass buckle from the Point. All parade and morning report." He gave a dry laugh that seemed half alkali and sand. "Be a miracle if he knows the manual of arms."

"You oughtn't to say that," Huston said, and then paused. He wished now that he had let it be; it was wrong that Muller should abuse his mind with wild, angry judgments. "You can't tell too much about him yet. In his own way, he may be very capable."

"Uh-huh. Reconnoitering."

"Well, it's a start, son, it's a start. It's in the right direction." Then, all at once, Huston felt impatient with Muller; he felt it in the same way that he would, had Muller been his son, Charley. "What would *you* do?" he asked.

Muller didn't seem to have an answer for that. Tipping his head to the side, he looked upward toward the trees that hung over the tanks. For a moment, and as though some old memory was stirred by what he saw up there, a light came into his eyes.

"My old squad . . ." he said; then began again, "my old squad . . ."

It wasn't clear though what his old squad would do. He stopped, and when the light left his eyes, he slid again to the earth. With his hands against his face, he shook his head, as though that would help him finish it. All that followed though was, "It wouldn't stop with any goddamn reconnoitering."

After that he leaned back and closed his eyes against the wide glare of sky and earth. Huston, as he watched, could feel a complication of emotions come over him. In some ways, he was thinking, Muller was hard to like; but then he wondered how much different he would be himself if he'd set out on such a course and had it all go to smash. Then, more than ever, he was aware of the identity he saw in Muller. So he pitied him the cause of his unhappiness, and this warring with himself and the others with him.

Muller had deserted from the Army, and yet he still retained a feeling for his old unit. He had run a grave risk in order to marry a girl, who he hoped was waiting for him; but having done so, it was plain that he was no longer certain of his love for her. In provoking him, she'd made a question of his confidence in her.

To Huston, it looked plain enough. Coming from the coach, he'd heard enough to piece together what he hadn't heard. It was a sorry way to end things for Muller, if things were nearing an end. And it was enough to make him think that Muller should have a chance to set himself to rights.

11.

"God in heaven," Miss Hale said, "why can't that rain come here?"

It was the first time she'd spoken since arriving at the rock, and it was less a question asked of some person than of the sky itself, or of the world, or of God.

Along with all of the others, except for Patterson, who still was reconnoitering, and Wagner, who lay asleep, Huston leaned against the rock and watched the cloud for some sign of coming near them. It was as big a cloud as he had ever seen in this country, and filled the whole southern sky above the Catalinas with its swollen blackness. Still it rose and spread above the mountains, swelling into high anvils as it did this time of day in summer, flat and white on the great height of their tops, and dark and bellied with its moisture at the deep lower levels. Sometimes, as he watched the various parts of the vast main mass form and shape themselves, Huston saw the glow of lightning in their caverns and crevasses; and at the base of the cloud there came to be long shades of slowly changing gray that would be rain descending on the high peaks of the mountains.

The cloud spread over a range of many miles, ranging east and west of the Catalinas; and over on the western edge of it, the sun had filled the moving curtains with a yellow light, so that he knew the rain that now fell out of it was partly dust stirred out of the desert to the west; and that the great winds coming from within the cloud were beginning to drive the storm across the sandy valley toward Tucson.

Whether or not the rain would come to them eventually, he could not yet tell. In its growth, the cloud had swelled and spread in their direction; but save a high, outflung edge, which nearly reached them but not quite, the Tortolitas had no immediate indication of rain nearing. About all you could say for where they were was that the rock was not so flaming any more, and that the shadow had extended. It must have moved a number of feet, and now he wondered how much time had gone by since they had come. Just sitting, waiting while they watched the cloud to see if it was coming closer, it was hard to tell.

"I don't see why it can't come here," Miss Hale said, still speaking in the same way as before.

"It don't do any good to gab at it," Jager said to her.

"I'm not gabbing at it. I'm just asking, that's all."

"Well, that don't help none, either," Jager said.

She didn't answer that time, but turned again to the cloud, her expression such that Huston did not like to look at it, or at the cloud, either.

He looked away from both, and took his watch from his pocket. It said a little after five, and they might have been here for half an hour. He began to put it away, but when his glance passed over Wagner, he thought better of it and crossed the few yards lying between them on his knees and took Wagner's wrist in one hand while he watched the dial face. Then he studied the flush on Wagner's face, and the bluish tint beginning to show beneath his fingernails. The pulse was high, and that could be expected; but the flush was normal for the heat and strain, and the blue had just started. He would probably have a headache when he wakened, but he was not in any immediate danger. Wagner was a tough old man.

Still, was he to go now, it would be the way, quiet and in his sleep, knowing that he'd been able to do what he'd intended to do.

It was after Huston sat down again that he felt Miss Hale watching him. She had shifted, as though observing the cloud was too despairing to keep up for any length of time; and she was looking at him in a grave manner.

"You're a doctor, aren't you?" she said.

"Why do you say that?" Huston said, although it was logical that she guess before the others did. Women were more observing of detail than were men. But he would rather not talk about his being a doctor.

The girl shrugged her shoulders, and he was aware of thinking that she did it as a girl of her kind would. Then he knew it was an error to think of her as being of a certain kind, even though his being with her through the day had told him things.

"The way you did that," she said. "That and the

stones back there. You spoke to Joseph, too, about his bottle."

"I used to be a doctor; not any more," Huston said.

"You don't have a practice now?"

"No," he said, "not now," although that wasn't really true. He had practiced a year in Cincinnati, half a year in Buffalo, another year in Kansas City, a scatter of years in Minnesota, Pennsylvania, Iowa, Missouri, and in between, any number of odd months as a contract surgeon for the Army, or for Indian agencies in the West.

"I see," she said, and after a long pause she went on again, but slower. "I was wondering if you knew how long we could last."

"Here?" he said, and when she nodded he was conscious of the others. He could not remember Wagner waking when he took his pulse, but he was not sleeping now. Jager turned to look at him, and Muller, too. They all were listening, and it was strange, as if each responded to his name. But that was how it went when death was brought up.

"Why, it more or less depends," he said; and now he wondered if they really wanted to know, or if it was related to that morbid fascination which death had for humans.

Well, he knew how it would go, and they were well started by now. He knew the symptoms; he could feel them in himself, and had for some

135

time. You began with thirst, the easiest to notice. Then your skin grew flushed and you became sleepy. After a time you discovered that your appetite was gone, and you might be sick to your stomach; though so far, at least, no one had been nauseated. Motion became a chore; and if you took your pulse, it would be higher than normal.

In a while now the headaches and the dizziness would begin; you came to notice that your arms and legs tingled, and that your breath was short, as though you had been running hard or climbing. You would not be able to spit at all, and when you spoke, the words would be fuzzy. When you walked, if you had strength enough to walk by that time, you would not be able to walk as you wished. By now they had a little of that behind them, too.

The last phase, if you could neatly break it down in that way, was ruthless and swift. You were deafened, but you still could hear a wide variety of sounds—distant roarings, bells, human speech, choirs singing in remote, unknown churches. Your vision dimmed, but you saw people that you knew, houses that you might have lived in, cities. Your skin numbed and shriveled, and when you urinated, if you still could by that time, it would be a painful business.

It was now that you ran toward the lakes of fine blue waters, or threshed your way toward castles on the mountains, or tried to dig for water through solid rock.

There would be variations, depending on the person, of course; but the end would be the same. And when your body gave up fighting there would be the great birds soaring in the sky, and little animals coming out of their burrows, waiting their turn at table.

He hadn't thought of it in such a wealth of detail before. He felt carried away by the illusion, and when it left him he felt a mild surprise to find that he was still at the rock. But it was there, pressing at his back. The others, Miss Hale, the men, were there, too.

Jager said, "Depends? On what?" while they waited for him.

Huston blinked at Jager. He was still returning from his illusion. It was the first time that Jager seemed to have an interest in what was going on.

"Why," Huston began again, "motion, for one thing."

"You mean, if you're quiet, you last longer than moving?"

Huston nodded. "Yes, it works along those lines."

"How long, then, if we just sit here, like we are now?"

"Oh, three days perhaps, at these temperatures," Huston said, although he knew it would not be anything like that. But it had just come over him that all they had was hope, and he could not destroy that for them. He didn't mind the truth himself, but it wouldn't do the others much good.

"Otherwise?" Jager said.

"Less," Huston said. "Maybe two."

Miss Hale let her face down into her hands, and when she raised it she had turned again to watch the cloud.

"Don't forget about that," she said.

"About what?" Jager said.

"The cloud," Miss Hale said. "It could reach us yet. It's got plenty of rain for us, if it does. I think the edge has come closer while we've been sitting here."

Everybody now looked at the cloud again, and held their silence while they tried to see if Miss Hale was right or not. Jager sat against the rock and stared out impassively. Muller sighted on the cloud, trying to line up various parts of it upon the mountain peaks. Even Wagner rolled over, then he got his elbows under him and pushed up.

Whether or not the cloud had neared more, Huston could not tell. The edge was almost overhead, as it had been, but he could not judge its movement. And even if it did reach over them, it occurred to him that they would still be in the position of lying under the outer edge of a funnel, with all the moisture draining toward the center, which lay over the Catalinas, and now, to some extent, above the valley where Tucson lay. He did not feel very hopeful about rain; still, she *might* be right about the outward spreading of the edges.

"It doesn't look to me like it has," Jager said.

"Well, it has," Miss Hale said. "That little part of it up there has come closer."

She bent her head to look above, but after Jager looked he shook his head.

"I still don't see it," he said, and more definite this time, as though disappointing Miss Hale was more important to him than what the cloud did.

"You just don't want to see it, Ansel, that's all."

"How would that have anything to do with it?" Jager said with a snort.

"It has a lot to do with it, and you know why, too."

"My God, you either see it or you don't," Jager said, "and I don't."

"You would, if you wished to," she said, and she was very close to tears again when Muller spoke up.

"Why, it might have moved a little, at that," he said, though Huston had the notion that he said it only as a comfort to Miss Hale.

She smiled at him. Then she said to Jager, "There, I'm not the only one who sees it. Joseph sees it, too, and if you wished to, so would you. You don't, just because I do. That's the way it is."

Then she did begin to cry; and as everybody knew that the cloud was only a part of the reason, there was no more to be said. So they turned from her to the south, as if each was suddenly taken with the chance that rain was coming nearer, after all.

It only lasted for a moment. Then, as if playing out the fairy tale of hope for long enough, Muller got to his feet.

"What are you going to do?" Huston said. "You'd better save your strength and sit down."

"I've been hearing that all day," Muller said, holding to the rock and looking around him. "I'm going to look for a barrel. There ought to be a barrel around here somewhere."

"A what?" Huston said.

"A barrel, a bisnaga," Muller said, standing in his ill-fitting clothing while he looked around.

Huston remembered what it was then; the second name had told him. The bisnaga was a barrel-shaped cactus that had a storage basin just above the root system. Sometimes, when it was opened with a knife or ax, a bitter, milky fluid could be found in it. He had seen none of them coming over, and he said so to Muller.

"Neither did I," Muller said, "but we wasn't looking for one, neither."

He started moving off, holding to the rock to keep himself steady. When he was gone Huston saw Jager grinning at him.

"There goes the man who believed in rain," he said. "Finding a barrel, what he called it, has the same chance."

Hearing that, Miss Hale looked up and it was plain to see that she had just begun to get the meaning of Muller's errand. Had he really believed in the cloud, he would have stayed. In a glance, she looked above, and in turn at Jager and Huston, and Huston knew that he disliked Jager still more than earlier. There would be a streak of sadist in him, too.

"We're pretty dependent on chances now," he said. "We can't afford to overlook any that might show promise."

He stopped, knowing he had not been much help; and then another thought occurred to him, and he leaned toward Miss Hale.

"There's a chance we might be found," he went on, although he felt that chance was just as slender as the rain or Muller's barrel.

Miss Hale did not answer right away, but Jager seemed to find it interesting.

"Why do you say that?" asked the gambler with an edge that made Huston draw up in his mind. He had only thrown it out as something that they might hang onto, especially the girl; now he had to think.

"Well, the eastbound ought to be along before long," he said. "Once they see the wreckage, they'll look for tracks leaving it."

"Why, yes, that's so," the girl said. "That could happen."

"I wouldn't be counting on it," Jager said, as if it was poor policy to place hope in that, too. "They don't run but once a week, either way; and the eastbound passed through Tucson only a couple of days ago."

"It could happen though," Huston said, and he was aware of putting weight behind the words. He looked a little harder at Jager. "There's a chance of it."

Jager wouldn't allow that to stand. He seemed bent upon destroying whatever hope was held.

"Even so," he said, "I wouldn't count on it. You're only getting your hopes up, that's all."

"What's wrong with hope?" Huston said; and in saying that, he became aware, all at once, of the inconsistency of his thought. Before, he hadn't thought in terms of chances, or of hope, at all; and one way or the other he had looked upon the eventual outcome of this thing as foreordained. Now, however, it surprised him that he did not find that end so acceptable to him as it had been earlier.

Then, as Jager looked away again, something else occurred to Huston. This surprised him, too, coming at him all at once, as a sudden beam of light in his mind. It was ugly, and he tried to push it away, but it would not stay away. It kept coming back, and as he looked at Jager's lean face, it was hard to keep from wondering why Jager would rather not be found.

12.

Muller found no barrel cactus. When he returned in fifteen or twenty minutes, he did not have to tell them, for his face showed it, and when he sank to the earth below the rock no one asked him about it.

Shortly after this, Lieutenant Patterson came back. He had been gone a longer time than Muller, and he dragged himself around the shoulder of the rock and threw himself upon the ground. He lay there for some time while the breath pumped in and out of him in a heavy rasping sound.

Finally he sat up and hitched himself against the rock and took off his cap. Removed, it left a red line across his forehead like a bullet crease.

"Well, they are there, all right," he said when he had breathed for several more seconds.

"You see 'em?" Wagner said, pushing up on his elbows and speaking for the first time in a great while.

"Not the Indians," Patterson said. "I saw a horse standing in the trees. It was only a glimpse but enough to know."

"I knowed it," Wagner said, as if the pleasure of being right was bigger in him than the meaning of it.

"What are you going to do about it, now you

know?" Muller said. "No doubt you got that figured out, too."

"There's nothing funny about our situation, Muller," Patterson said to him.

"I ain't said there was," Muller said. "A fellow like you should have the answer though."

Muller had gone to find a barrel, but his failure now seemed less important to him than that he chivvy Patterson about his reconnoitering. He sat on the ground against the rock and grinned at him.

"If an answer is all you want, you might consider the marked resemblance between the situation here and that at Borodino," the Lieutenant said. "But then I'm sure you've noticed."

"Yah?" Muller said.

Huston smiled, and felt his head move in a slow shake. Borodino had been fought in Russia more than fifty years ago, while the Napoleonic wars were devastating Europe. The turning point of the battle came when a lofty earthen redoubt, on which the Russian cannon had been placed, was taken. Borodino was a victory for the French, but winning had cost Napoleon more than thirty thousand men, many of them falling at the redoubt. It was long ago and half a world away, but it was hardly odd that Patterson should see the similarity. That was how his mind would work.

However, it was doubtful whether Muller had

even heard of Borodino. He said, "Yah?" again, while trying to get his mind around it. He looked up the slope. Then, as if it was a cue, all eyes turned upward. In the heavy, drowning heat, the trees were still and green, but Huston could imagine the Apaches lying in their shelter while they watched.

"I wonder if they're the same that made the coach go over," Miss Hale said in a while.

"They could be," Huston said. "I think we would have seen them though, coming over."

"Likely a hunting party," Wagner said. "Stopped for water first; then, seein' us, they figured to wait."

"I don't see it makes much difference what they are," Jager said. "They're all alike, for my money."

"There's a difference in their arrows," Muller said, "and what they can do to you."

Patterson turned to look at Muller. "There is?" he said, to make it plain that it was new to him.

"You mean you didn't *know* that?" Muller said, and then he laughed and said, "Hell, I thought you knew everything."

On hearing that, Lieutenant Patterson held himself quite still for a moment, and everybody else grew watchful in the sudden quiet. A line that Huston hadn't seen before ran through his mouth from side to side, thin and straight. He leaned toward Muller.

145

"I know what I've been taught," he said, "and I'm able to learn more. And from the look of you, that's more than you can say."

"You don't know your way up that old hill though," Muller said.

Muller was leaning back against the rock and smiling with a hard light in his face. He looked alert and watchful, but that he might be nearing dangerous ground did not seem to matter to him. Taking on this way seemed to be a thing that he was driven toward, and Huston had the feeling that he was watching something that must run its course; something in the way of a natural process, like the running of the seasons.

"Maybe I don't yet," Patterson said, "but I hope to learn a way in time."

"In time?" Muller said, and he laughed. "That's wonderful. I guess that fixes everything. All we got to do is wait for you to get inspired. Given we don't die off first, that is."

"You don't have to wait on me for anything," Patterson said. "There's nothing I can think of that should hold you back from going up there yourself. Don't think I intend to stand in the way of your doing so."

"Why," Muller said, "you ought to know I wouldn't do a thing like that. Being in command, you ought to be the one to show us how to get up there. Was I to go ahead of you, I'd be guilty of insubordination."

"By God, Muller, I resent that! Not once have I presumed to take command of this party!"

"Lord to God, man, you been doin' it since we started out! We've hardly had a moment's peace from your telling us what we ought to do, or oughtn't to do. You even walked in front of us all."

Muller was standing now, against the rock, and the light of his smile was even brighter than it had been. That Patterson should admit that he did not know how to reach the water just now gave Muller an opportunity to avenge himself for all the ills that he believed the Army had worked on him. He was enjoying it very much, and yet Huston could not help but think that it was partly due to what he felt about the fact of his desertion.

It was natural for a man to place the reasons for his sins upon some other person, just as it was natural for a guilty man to charge another with his own crimes.

Patterson now was standing, too, and he had brought his face in on a level with Muller's.

"I don't know what's eating on you, Muller, but I'm not going to argue with you any longer. I don't argue strategy with civilians."

"I guess I got a right to argue when we've got our lives to think of here, and the only chance for water is up that hill!"

"Don't imagine I'm not thinking of our lives,"

Patterson said, "but only a fool would try to make it up that open slope in broad daylight."

"Maybe it ain't so much a matter of foolishness as you'd like to have us think," Muller said.

Muller was grinning very broadly now, and Huston knew that things had reached a point that went beyond the earlier quarrels and arguments. He could feel it as a quality in the air, just as he could feel the pressing moistness of the cloud above them.

The cloud was in his mind when he stepped between them, trying to force them back from each other.

"Now, now," he said, "this is no good. This is no good at all. Let's see some sense from you two now."

He put his hands against their chests and tried to push them back, but they ignored him and would not move.

"By God," Patterson said to Muller, "you're calling me a coward!"

"Speakin' of it's your idea, not mine," Muller said.

"Men! Men!" Huston said, pushing again upon their chests. "This quarreling is all needless. Almost any minute now it's going to rain. Look at the sky, if you will."

It was not exactly true about the rain. If anything, the edge of the cloud appeared to be in motion, almost imperceptibly, toward the west. But you would never notice it unless you were diverted from looking at it steadily. The quarrel had done that, and as he now saw the change, Huston wished he had been slower to interrupt the argument by calling attention to it.

But now the others saw it, and all at once they grew quiet while they looked above. They all looked, staring with their faces turned upward. Close to a minute passed before they could be sure the edge was raveling off to the west.

Then Muller spoke the dreadful truth.

"It isn't going to rain. The cloud is moving away."

They stood there with their cracked lips and scalded faces lifted, trying not to believe what he'd said; but it was so.

"Oh," Miss Hale said in a soft breath of sound. "Oh, oh."

"I told you not to get excited over it," Jager said.

Wagner did not speak; and Patterson only glanced above, and down again, as if the meaning it conveyed to him was less to him than that Muller should impugn his courage.

"By God, sir," he said to Muller, "I'm awaiting your apology."

"Now, now," Huston said, "there is still a good chance for rain. The airs will likely shift again."

"Not from me, you don't get one," Muller said

to Patterson. "Being a coward was your idea, not mine. I said nary a word."

Huston tried again to push between the two men, but they were too close now. "Good heavens, men. Give the rain a chance," he said.

"Goddamn it, Muller," Patterson said, "I'd call you out for satisfaction, if you were in the Army! But I demean myself by even talking to you. I demean the honor of every soldier in the Army by talking to you!"

"What?" Muller said. "What?" he said again; and he came forward even more, his mouth made into a curl that was very different from the smile.

"I demean the honor of every man in uniform by talking to a tramp of your kind," Patterson said. "A creature such as you are would not be allowed on post, even to clean the latrines!"

"By God!" Muller said. Then he shouted, "By God! You call yourself a soldier! You stand there telling me about the Army, and you call yourself a soldier! You don't know what soldiering is!"

Muller was shouting even louder now. He stretched his eyes and waved his arms in the air, and Huston had to back a step to keep from being hit by one of his wild swings. It was plain that Muller's rage with Patterson, together with his anger with himself, was getting the better of what judgment he had left.

All the same, Huston tried still another time to push between them; but he ran into one of

Muller's arms and stumbled back. Muller pushed his face ahead and raised his voice to a bawl.

"By God, you don't know what soldiering is! You don't even know where soldiering begins!" He waved his arms at the slope, and Huston knew that all restraint had left him, and that pride in what he once had been was all that he could think of now. "Goddamn it, my old squad would be up there and back again two times over by now!"

He finished in a wild shout, his mouth still gaping and his arms flung in mid-air when he stopped. Then it was as if some tiny grain of sense had found a chink through which to enter his rage, and he drew back a step. But he had let it out, or he had let something out, and Patterson made a leap in his mind to the meaning.

In a breath that left him in a rush, he said, "So!"

He stared at Muller, at his poorly fitting clothes, at the weathered color of his face; as though he saw them for the first time in relation to all that Muller had let on to know about the country, and Muller's endless railing against the Army.

"So!" he said again, and it was now as though everything had come together in a pattern that he could understand. "I thought there was something queer about you. You're a deserter! That's what you are, a common deserter!"

Whatever Muller might have thought he was, it was plain that he had not considered himself in any such bald and harsh terms.

"What?" he said. "What?"

"I called you a deserter," Patterson said again. "And that's exactly what you are, a common, filthy deserter!"

"I ain't!" Muller said, and now his eyes grew rounder while the knowing grew bigger in him. "I ain't!" he said, this time in a high shout, as if saying it enough, and loud enough, would make the meaning go away. "I ain't! I ain't! I ain't!"

"You call me a coward," Patterson went on, "yet you lack even the rudimentary guts to finish your enlistment."

"Goddamn it," Muller yelled, "I ain't!"

Patterson now smiled at Muller. Then he laughed, leaning over and slapping his leg with his hand.

"Oh, by George, that's good," he said. "A common deserter setting the standards of courage for the Army; a man who slinks and sneaks away for want of the simple guts to serve his time. Oh, that's a good one."

He laughed again while Muller stared at him. Muller's face now looked like he had never spent a day in the out-of-doors. There was around his eyes a kind of numb, unseeing look, as if all that Patterson said had struck him for the first time, and like an ax. It was easy to see that it had never occurred to him before.

"By Christ!" he said, and he stared around him, as a blind man might stare in trying to see,

152

seeking some denial; but there seemed to be no way to turn it away from him. Everyone was watching him, but there was nothing they could say. Even Huston, now that it had come to this point, could think of nothing.

"By Christ," Muller said again. His eyes came back to Patterson, then passed him and went up the slope and after they had searched the trees they returned to Patterson. There was now a change of some kind, but Huston was too slow to catch it right off.

"By God, it's guts you want, is it?" Muller said. He took a step between them, and after he had passed them he looked back. "Goddamn it, come with me if you're so gutty, Patterson. I'll show you something about guts!"

"Joseph!" It was Miss Hale, as though she knew ahead of them all what Muller was planning to do.

Huston caught it then, and stretched out and tried to reach for Muller as he went by. "Sit down," he called out, and he reached again; but Muller had now passed and got around him. He was moving away from them toward the slope.

"Joseph!" Miss Hale called a second time. "Joseph! Come back!"

But Muller did not stop, nor did he turn back. He was staring straight ahead of him; and when Huston tried to get his hands on him again, Muller slapped them down and kept moving out.

13.

Huston tried again, reaching in a wild stretch that left him flat and sprawled across the ground; but it was no good. Muller was out of the shelter of the rock before he could be stopped, and stepping on the rise that went up the slope. A number of yards in front of it, he tripped and stumbled to his knees. Scrambling after him, Huston got his hands upon him, but Muller had a strength and will that Huston could not hold, and when he jerked away from him he staggered to his feet and lunged on.

Now in the sunlight, Muller's pistol appeared in his hand and flickered in the brightness. He was running, running as a gut-shot deer will run when life is leaving it and there is nothing left for it to go on but the reflex of its wildness. Against the glaring wideness of the white slope, he looked small and dark, and as he ran on with that senseless drive, it seemed to Huston that he saw himself in his place. It was happening as he had imagined it would happen when he had thought of going up there; and when the arrow came there was a moment when it seemed to him that it was going through his own body. Muller was transfixed, but Huston could feel the arrow in himself.

In a single second, he could see the sunlight on the thin, reaching streak, and then the streak becoming one with Muller. With a part of his mind he could see the blur of dark face that came and went inside the stone slot beneath the trees, the menace of the moving line, and Muller turning with the arrow in his shoulder, throwing out his arms wide, while his revolver circled in the air and his shout went out in wild echoes against the planes of the mountain.

That was when Huston heard another shout, his own. It was different when he heard himself, and he knew that what had happened was not any kind of vision. Muller was on his back, lying with the arrow sticking high up from his body, and Huston was running toward him. He could hear somewhere a shout from Patterson. Then, together with the shout, he heard the shot that Patterson fired, and felt the wide concussion blast that slapped across his shoulders.

But it was all run together in his mind: the running, the Lieutenant firing at the trees above the tanks, the shouting and his stumbling up the slope. It seemed to take a long, long while, but when he got to Muller he knew it hadn't taken any time at all because the arrow, as it stood up, still trembled with its spent life.

The shaft was very long, and at the nock had three feathers; from what he knew of them, it would ordinarily be a hunting arrow. To see it shiver in that way, as though its work was not yet finished, made him want to seize it and jerk it out; but he was afraid to touch it so soon. All around the haft, the red blood welled up in bubbles that shone and rounded in the sun until they broke and spilled down over the stained cloth of Muller's wet shirt. His face had gone a clear white beneath his deep tan, and his eyes were closed tightly. His lips were pale and twitching in a way that made it seem as though a cry was struggling to break through his unconsciousness.

Coming up to Muller, Huston saw it all in a glance. Then he dropped to his knees at Muller's head and put his hands beneath his shoulders. Patterson was standing over them with the revolver aimed at the tanks above. Huston yelled at him.

"Take his feet!" he shouted. "Hurry! Take his feet!"

"Drag him down!" Patterson shouted, and fired again at the slot beneath the trees. "Drag him down! I'll keep you covered!"

"Cover be damned!" Huston shouted. "Take his feet, man! Dragging him will kill him!"

"No quicker than these Indians!" Patterson said, and fired again. "Start dragging him!"

As there was no sense in going on in that way, Huston started dragging Muller down the slope. Bending down to put his back into the work, he caught a glimpse of Jager below them on level ground with his pistol drawn. He was beginning to send a covering fire over them at the tanks, but he was keeping in the shelter of the rock.

Huston heaved, feeling Muller's weight. As Jager fired, Patterson turned to see where the shot was coming from.

"For Christ's sake, will you come?" Huston shouted at him. "We're covered from below! Take his feet, man!"

Patterson did, that time, what he was asked; he leaned and lifted Muller's feet, and they began the slow move downward over the stony rough ground. Huston staggered under the dead weight, his legs and arms trembling.

They went slowly down the pitch of the grade while Jager fired around and over them at the tanks. The arrow, standing upright, shivered with their jolting motion, while the blood pumped out of the wound. Sometimes it would form a puddle in a fold in the cloth of Muller's shirt, and when the fold was filled, the blood would spill over and drain to the ground.

Huston did not like to watch it, but he watched because he could not make himself stop; it was too much like a part of himself. He knew the artery had been pierced, and that there wasn't very much time. He would watch the blood, gleaming crimson in the bright sunlight; then he would look down, ahead of them, and try to measure the distance left. It was hard to believe that Muller had got so high on the slope so quickly, that the rock was still so far.

Then the blood would draw his eye again, willy-nilly, and he would wonder if he would be able to stop the flow in time without proper instruments. He had never thought to take them from the boot when they had left the coach, and a fine place for them now, it was.

Finally they were there. Just when it began to seem that Muller's awkward weight would tear him loose from Huston's grasp, the slope lost its pitch in level ground and the high rock rose over them. Jager stepped aside to let them by him to its shelter. The girl ran forward, helping with the shifting weight of Muller as they lowered him.

"Oh," she said, "oh," the sound in a soft cry as they set him on the earth. "Oh, that wicked arrow."

Putting his pistol into his belt, Jager paused and half turned as if he had been pulled by her tone.

"He asked for it," he said. "He had it coming to him."

The girl did not answer Jager, and had only the side of her glance for him as she bent above Muller; but the words set Patterson off.

"He's a fool," he said, standing straight again from letting Muller's feet down. "A damned fool."

Huston got up slowly, feeling the weight that hung on in his arms and legs and back. He rolled his sleeves up while he studied Muller on the ground at his feet. But he had heard Patterson.

"He couldn't help it," he said. "He had many things on his mind."

"A damned fool, all the same. And a fine jam he nearly got us into, going up there. He could have got us all killed."

"Maybe," Huston said. He was feeling for his penknife in his pockets, wondering if he had lost it. He wished Lieutenant Patterson would go away. "I doubt he planned to."

The Lieutenant's voice began to grow louder now. He did not go away, but stood in front of Huston. "Maybe not," he said. "I'd hardly put it past him, however. He's a damned deserter, isn't he? And anyway, did he think he could make it up there all the way by himself?"

Huston found the knife and it was in his hand now. It was all he had to work with. The last time, he had wanted for skill and knowledge, and had failed for their lack; this time it was a matter of simple carelessness. Leaving his kit in the coach could mean the difference between life and death for Muller. The fault was his, of course, but Patterson made it easy to turn it onto him.

"Maybe he didn't think so," Huston said. "He tried to get there though. And, as I recall, you had an invitation from him."

Patterson's mouth fell open, but no words came forth. He simply stood there like a boy discovered

159

in the bushes with the neighbor girl. Even as he spoke, Huston knew that he was unfair, for there had been a kind of desperate quality to Muller's act.

But he knew he could not change the words once they were out. Nor could anything change the thoughts which passed through Patterson's eyes and away so swiftly. He would like to tell him that he was sorry, but he knew that would not make much difference.

Still silent, Patterson turned and moved off. Huston bent his knees and let himself down to the ground beside Muller. The girl was holding Muller's head, waiting for him to begin. Huston turned out the blade of his pocketknife with his thumbnail, and began to cut the shirt away from the shaft.

It was over now. Huston settled back and laid his knife on a piece of Muller's shirt. He brought his knees toward his chest, crossed his arms upon them and let his head down. It seemed to take a long time.

He breathed, going deep with each breath; and there was blood and sweat in it. The blood was Muller's and it pulled upon the fine hairs of his arms while drying. The sweat was his, and now he was surprised to find himself soaked in it. It was hard to believe that he'd had that much left in him.

He had though, and he was now weaker for its loss.

Sitting there, taking the air in heavy drags, and feeling the sweat upon him like a small rain, he could feel the shimmering of his nerves and muscles under his skin. The fatigue and wear were of the kind he might have suffered had he crossed again from the coach.

It was all finished; and if doing the job meant anything, he had done it well enough, without his instruments. He could tell, simply by the way the brain and fingers worked together; and he supposed that he could be proud of that. If surgery alone should decide, Muller had a fair chance.

Still, as if to make sure that all had gone the way it should have gone, his mind went on searching and pecking through little details.

He could still see it all clearly—the arrow sticking up and his cutting the shirt away. The girl had held Muller's head, and she had taken off a petticoat that could be torn up for bindings. When the moment came to push the arrow through, Huston had called for one of the men to steady Muller; but Miss Hale would not let go.

"Please," she said to Huston, as though it was a prime wish that she stay, "let me do it. I can hold him all right."

"He's going to jump," Huston said. "It's going to be a messy piece of work, too."

"I don't mind it though," Miss Hale said. "I

161

don't mind either one. I was raised in New York, in the slums . . ." as if this would not come up to things that might have happened there.

"You'd better let me do it," Jager said, though not as if he had Miss Hale's sensibilities in mind; but more as though he simply wished to get her away from Muller.

She seemed to know it, too, for when she shook her head at him it was a slow shake, the kind that might be meant to cover more than just this one thing. And it sounded in her voice—when she spoke.

"No," she said to him, "I'm going to do it, Ansel. He needs a woman now; and whatever else I may be, or may not be, I'm still a woman."

That settled it for Jager, and he drew off, his long face in stiff planes. The Lieutenant, who had lingered on the edge as if feeling he also should offer help, now moved away, still smarting from Huston's scolding.

After that was settled, and with no more delay, Huston cut the shaft above the hafting, pulled the blade clean out and then withdrew the shaft. To do this he got on his knees and put as much of his weight as he could upon Muller's shoulder so the arrow would go through quickly and clean.

All the while, the girl held Muller down, setting her weight to bear upon the other shoulder and across his chest. Huston was aware of wondering if she would go faint at what would happen next.

But she didn't; she held herself, and she held onto Muller, too; no matter how he bucked and squalled through his unconsciousness, nor how his stomach upchucked through the stroke of pain, nor how the blood came up like a fountain from the clear wound until the artery could be pressed—coming up and pouring down her front, her arms and hands, mixing with the mess that came from his stomach.

He could see himself, too, while he crouched above the arrow and felt the shiver of Muller's pain that traveled along its slender, delicate length. And he could see himself watching the red knife blade whittle the shaft through while he cursed its dullness; see his finger seek the artery under the slippery, crimson flesh; then hold it until the girl could fold the compress and bind it into place with the strips of cloth she had torn from her petticoat.

Then last, his belt came around and over Muller's chest to hold the bindings in place; and the sling, made of odds and ends of cloth, to hold the arm and to free the injured shoulder of weight.

Well, he had not done too badly. Not with what he'd had to work with. He'd done worse with more, at least once.

A little at a time, as if it was a thing to be considered well first, Huston brought up his head.

Muller lay the way he had been lying, his arms folded on his chest as for burial, a stain of blood in the white of the compress—not bad though; unless he had no more blood to lose. His face was getting some color, too, filling in the dirty white of the shock; and his breathing seemed more steady, though shallow.

He put his hand out, taking Muller's wrist in it. Under his fingers, he could feel the beat of Muller's heart—light and fairly rapid, yet not as rapid as it might have been. All things considered, it was not bad for now.

Then he knew his face had shown his satisfaction. Miss Hale had stopped her mopping with a piece of rag and was watching him.

"You're smiling," she said. "Does that mean good news?"

"I hope so," Huston said. "So far, he's holding his own."

Miss Hale moved her eyes from Huston down to Muller, and then off. They found the arrow, lying beyond in pieces.

"What about that? Don't they carry poison sometimes?"

Huston nodded. "Venom. Rattlesnake venom. Not on arrows for hunting though. I think Wagner's right about this crowd. If the blade was dipped, we'd know it by now."

As if the simple mention of it made the possibility acute, they both looked at Muller.

Thinking of it, however, Huston knew his fear of venom had been less than that of aloe. They used aloe, off and on, for hafting; when they wished the blade to loosen and the wound to suppurate. He must have spoken aloud.

"Aloe?" She looked up again; and when he had explained it, she moved her head.

"I've heard of it somewhere or other." She glanced at the knoll. "They're devils, aren't they? To think of such things."

"We like to think so," Huston said.

But you could tell that she would rather not think too long about that, for she was busy mopping once more, cleaning Muller off the best way she could. Without water, it was slow and hard work, but women had been dealing with the body's filth and refuse since man's time began upon earth.

When Huston had watched her for a while, he said, "You ought to let me do some of that."

She smiled, glancing at him while she worked on, but saying, "No, thanks, I'll do it. You've done plenty already. I don't mind it. No one ever got hurt by a little mess."

It was what he'd thought she'd say. Louise had been that way too.

She went on. "Women are used to messy work; they do it better than men do, too. Think of all the floors scrubbed, and all the clothes washed, and diapers changed never-ending, you might say."

She turned the cloth in her hand, finding a cleaner surface. "No, I don't mind it any. It gives me something to do."

But Huston knew it was more than that to her. Through the day, off and on, he'd seen the way that trouble seemed to rest upon her, and he'd seen the current of malice that passed between her and Jager. But it was different with her now. The change was as you see in someone freed of such trouble, or of someone who had lost it in that of some other person. It could be that she had taken a shine to Muller; but on the other hand, at least for now, it seemed that he was like an instrument that had brought forth some quality that she had never known of until now—or, as if that quality had been long dead, and had come back to life again.

The sun was dying now, going out in a pillar of fire beyond a range of hills whose color gave them more the character of shadow or of smoke than something solid. Nearer, there were other hills that held their scarred and broken faces to the west, and seemed to glow in the change of light as they passed from rose to lavender, to purples and blues. Sometimes they seemed like great and strange animals from myths and dreams; and yet, seeing their ragged, dun-stained flanks go softly colored with an inner light, it was easy to think that they possessed a kind of secret life, lived only at this hour. According to the Indians, they had such a life. And it was the time of evening, he recalled, that certain of the red men held the spirits of the mountains to be particularly active.

It was quiet now, too. Perhaps it had been quiet all the while, but in the evening quiet was more apparent than it might be at other times. Down to the south above the Catalinas and Tucson, there was still the thundering, heavily laden storm, the massive, high cloud stitched and ribbed with lightning, and the leading edge of the cloud still luminous with sundown; but that part which they had watched and gauged with so much hope had gone drifting still farther west. Over beyond him, the skinny branch of an ocotillo moved, but he could neither hear nor feel the air move. And still beyond, a kangaroo rat poked up out of a tumble of prickly pear; but it was gone without a sound, or even gone before he could be really certain that he had seen it at all.

Everything was silent in this hour of the day's end. The land lay quiet and at peace. You would think that sound was something that had gone to another part of the world.

The little group was quiet, too, lying or sitting on the ground. Huston noticed that Wagner hadn't moved since Muller had been carried off the hill, and lay sleeping once more. Leaning on the rock, the Lieutenant watched the shadows that formed about the trees and the tanks. Jager watched the storm, sitting quiet and at ease. You might think the heat had not worked very much upon him. Watching him—silent, for the most part, and withdrawn—you might even think that he was saving himself for something that the rest of them did not know of.

The first star now shone, the evening star, bright in the west beyond the fringe of cloud. Lieutenant Patterson stood away from the rock and came over toward Miss Hale and Muller and Huston.

"How is he?" asked the West Pointer.

"He's alive," Huston answered.

Patterson came nearer by another yard. "Can you tell yet if he's going to make it?"

"Can't tell too much yet. Fifty-fifty perhaps."

Patterson let the leavings of his boot bore at a stone while his eyes searched over the earth. Huston did not encourage him. He had got over feeling sorry for Patterson.

"I suppose it's my fault that he's lying there," Patterson said in the quiet.

As he made a question of it, Huston thought at first to answer, yes, it was; but now that he had thought about it for a time, he was no longer sure.

"No," he said in the pause. "Maybe not. Maybe he would have done it anyway. Sooner or later he might have taken the chance in any event."

"As he took the chance of deserting," the

Lieutenant said, as if it was the first thing in his mind, now that it appeared that he was not responsible.

"Perhaps," Huston said.

Huston glanced at Muller, knowing now that he had let Lieutenant Patterson too easily off the hook. Muller's color had deepened some, and he saw the beginning of fever in his face.

"He had the guilt of his desertion," Patterson said, sounding sure of himself again among the rules and regulations.

"And thirst." Huston settled his eyes on Patterson's face. "Don't forget that. Whatever else, he went up for water, too." He stopped, holding the last for a pause so that it would bear harder. Then he said, "And he needs it more now."

It was all changed again. As if pulled, Patterson's head began to turn, and when it faced the hill his glance went up to the trees above the stone tanks. In the last of daylight now, their tops were stained a greenish gold. All beneath their upper parts were lost in dark shadow, but the brilliance of the crowns told clearly of the water which fed the deep roots. Maybe more than when you saw them in the pallid glare of full daylight.

"I know," he said, still looking up, still held by the green-gold of the watered trees. "I know," he said again. Seemingly of its own mind, a hand crossed over and made a fist in the other; he started moving away. "We'll think of something," he said, and he was still looking up.

He went away, and then Miss Hale said, "Joseph's awake." Her hand came out to rest on Muller's forehead. "And warm, too."

"Yes," Huston said, "he'll run a fever, all right. But night should cool him off some."

Muller's eyes were now open, and heat and hurt were in the glassy whites. The pupils stared. In a breath, he said, "Water."

The girl smiled while she bent above him with her hand on his forehead. "There'll be water soon, Joseph. It won't be any time at all now."

Muller's eyes hitched, the focus coming and going in the hunt for her face. Then they settled on her and a smile began to work at his mouth.

She smiled upon him still, and in the softness of the twilight Huston wondered what had ever made him think of her as an ugly woman. Just now, in this moment that he watched her, she was beautiful, and it was more than what the colors of the evening might do. Her arms and clothes were stained with blood, the mess from Muller's stomach and the sweat of her own body; but she was beautiful even so, and there was quiet and radiance in her features.

For a moment, it made Huston wonder if she could be in love. The time that he had thought of anything like love was so far in the past and so remote to him that he no longer felt he recognized the true signs. But all at once he wanted her to be in love; or, rather, he wanted her to have the chance to be. He knew it was the place of idle fools to scheme and plan the lives of other people, but he was not planning anything; he did not mean anything like that. All he wished was that she have the chance, she and Muller, at least the chance.

It was very strange for him to have a thought of that kind, and then to stop and recognize it filled him with a driving fierceness. It startled him, because he hadn't known such thoughts or feelings for longer than he could think. Strangers to him, they came at him through the shifting grays of his long habit of indifference. They made him want to strike out, for the first time, at this impotence, at this being trapped, at this creeping death.

Then, to think of death in that way made him draw up in his thoughts and take a long look at it. When he had, he understood the change; and he understood, too, that he wished to live again, himself.

14.

It was good dark now, the stars like scratches of flame that were seen through a seedy blanket held up to a campfire. Off in the south, the lightning flickered and ran above the Catalinas, and now and then in the west, as the storm so moved. Sometimes there would be a light cast out of it that made it seem as if a stove door had been opened and then closed again, quick. Over toward the east, beyond the Tortolitas, the horizon was still dark, there being no sign yet of a moon; though an hour or so should see something of it.

Not that Jager felt he had to have a moon. He would be better off without it for the time being—anyway, until he got well away from this place. The North Star would be good enough for now, although the moon would help later on.

He got up slowly, easing himself to his feet. He was tired enough, and dry enough, but he had slid along through the afternoon and felt in fair shape. The money belt was dragging at his middle, and there was that other bulk beneath his armpit, as well; but they weren't so bad, not after sitting as quietly as he had. Anyway, one was the reason for his going; the other, the means.

Standing now, he leaned upon the rock a moment while he looked to see where everyone was. He didn't want to stumble over them on his way out in the dark.

From what he could tell, they seemed about the way they had been for the past hour, except for Patterson who, like a kid who is both scared and taken by a thing, had climbed on top of the high rock to watch the trees and tanks; for all the good it did him, or was likely to do. The others hadn't moved any though. Wagner lay asleep. Huston showed in a dark lump a few yards from Muller, another lump beneath the lighter mark of his bandage. Maggie was sitting next to him, bending over his face from time to time, the only one of them not sleeping or resting.

He would have moved off then, having got them placed, except that Maggie picked that time to bend her face again above Muller's. She did it like he was a child, or like they might have been lovers; and the sight held him there.

He watched, seeing her hand move over Muller's forehead, feeling the burn begin to fan up in him. He was finished with her, finished with her talk of marriage, and done with all of her talk and nagging over how he lived. Still, it burned, even so. It wasn't for her to say when it was over.

He saw her head bend down more, and then he felt his legs move. He had no thought to go to her, or to make a ruckus in his leaving, but what he saw there pulled at him, willy-nilly. She was his, by God; his, at least until he turned loose of her.

He was there, all at once, hardly knowing that he'd crossed the ground in between them.

Hearing his boot scrape, she put her head up. "Ans?"

"Yuh," he said, "it's me."

She sat straighter, as if she had a warning of his mood.

"What do you want, Ans?" She put her head up

still higher, trying to see some meaning in his face through the dark.

Jager wondered what he wanted. He wondered what he was doing here. He hadn't meant to get involved in anything.

When he didn't answer right away, she said, "What's the matter, Ans?" as though his being there meant that something had to be wrong. It wasn't so long since she'd been glad to have him with her, been begging for his attention.

Now, all at once, she wasn't; just his walking over meant something was the matter.

"I'm pulling out," he said, glad enough to let free of it, after all.

"What?" she said.

"I said, I'm pulling out. Now. I'm pulling for Picacho. I'm getting out of this place."

It was quiet while she thought about that. He tried to see her face, but in the dark he could not make it out. Then she said quietly, "Ans, I think you'd better sit down again."

Of all she might have said, he hadn't been ready to hear that. Maybe it wasn't in her any longer to plead with him about a thing, but he hadn't expected her to say a thing like that.

"I'm doin' it, goddamn it. I'm pulling out. I mean it."

But that made no difference, either. It was fixed in her mind that he was worn down by the heat.

"Ans, you better sit," she said, but softer this

time, so that it was quite plain what she was thinking.

"You'll never make it," someone said, and it was Huston butting in now. He stirred beyond, and slowly, pushing and hauling, sat up. "You'll never make it that far, Jager."

"Yes, I will," Jager said, knowing now that he was very close to telling his means. It burned in him, wanting to be loose; but he held onto it. "I'll make it, all right. It's cooling now."

"That doesn't make any difference," Huston said. "It's water you need for traveling; coolness won't help much now. Sit down, man, save your strength."

"Yes, Ans," Maggie said, and in the same way that she might say it to an idling boy, "do what he says. Please sit down."

Hearing her speak in that way made the thing he knew burn more than ever in him. That she should make it sound that he had lost his mind, and all the while be stroking the head of Muller, was more than he could bear. More than anything else, even more than getting away, he wished to hurt her.

He couldn't hold it in him any longer now, and it was time to let it out. "I've got water," he said.

"What?" and they spoke together.

"I've got water," he said again. "I've got the driver's water bottle."

Having said it now, having had it rip away

from him, he felt the way you do when you have set yourself upon some dangerous way from which there's no turning back. He felt the blood pour into his head, and a tingling prickled his skin.

"So, that's it," Huston said in the silence of their understanding of what he'd said.

"Give me that water bottle," Maggie said.

Jager moved backward a pace. Her voice surprised him; it was dead level in tone and full of menace. "No," he said, and now he knew that it had been an error coming over here, and an error telling her, no matter the pleasure it gave him.

Then a new thought came out of nowhere, and he heard his voice say, "You don't have no chance but me. If he gets the water, I don't reach Picacho. It's a trade of him for us. From his looks, he won't make it anyway."

"Give it to me," Maggie said again.

"No!" he said, and he was glad now that he'd told her, after all. "No!" he said in a shout, while the gladness came to a froth in his head. "He can rot, for all I care! All of you can rot!"

"You filth," Huston said. He began to rise, and Jager saw the gathering motion in the dark. "I thought you had something on your mind all along."

"I've got a gun here," Jager said. "Stand back."

"You excrement. You weeping sore."

176

From the top of the high rock, Patterson's voice called, "Ho, down there! Is anything wrong?"

"Stand back," Jager said again to Huston, but Huston wasn't standing back. He kept coming on, growing in the dark before him.

Jager would have liked to kill him, but the sound would be too great to take a chance of that kind. Maybe Patterson could shoot, and then again maybe not; but there was always luck. So he held himself in, and when he knew the range was right, he swung his pistol barrel at Huston's head, feeling it hit in a skid, but good enough to knock him over and down.

Somebody else was there, then, all at once, and it was Maggie. She came at him swift and silent, in the manner of some wild creature stalking prey; and save her breathing, no sound came from her. For a moment he was caught off balance by the jarring slam of her body. She swarmed upon him, swarmed all over him in that second of his first surprise. Her nails raked over his face, her knees drove into his crotch and her hands wrenched at his clothing while they tried to find the bottle slung under his shoulder.

She might have got it, too, so staggered was he by the sudden impact; but she stumbled in her high shoes, then she tripped herself in some way and lost her drive forward. Feeling her hands drag loose of his clothes, he got his feet to steady under him and gathered himself together. Staring

177

hard, he made her out as she began to fall, still silently; and when he brought his arm around, his fist was there in time to drive her into the earth at his feet.

Then he turned around and ran. Rounding the point of the high rock, he heard Patterson calling down again from on top.

"Ho, the ground!" he called. "What the devil's the noise about? Is everything all right?"

"Fine!" Jager shouted as he ran, knowing that the noise made no difference now. In the dark they wouldn't find him, nor would they dare to trail him. "Everything's fine, you witless bastard!"

He ran for twenty yards or so, slowed to a walk for half of that, and then ran again. After a minute or more of changing that way, running and slowing to walk, both, he stopped and he fell to his knees on the sand and stone of the desert floor.

Then, as if his hands belonged to someone else, perhaps to Maggie, they wrenched and jerked at the bottle under his coat. When freeing it, they jammed it into his mouth where his teeth clamped onto the neck.

He drank, the water plunging into his mouth in a foreign taste, and on down through his throat until it struck his stomach where it bucked and churned. He drank a long while, and not until the brassy taste of nausea came back up his throat and lay upon his tongue did he take the bottle from his mouth. Then, for a longer while he stayed there on his knees, carefully holding the bottle and trying to keep some kind of balance in his stomach. At first, it seemed that he might lose the water, but after a time of sitting as still as he knew how, and watching the stars in order to keep his mind away from it, he felt steadier.

Maybe he sat that way for five minutes, watching the stars and holding himself against his losing the water. Slowly it settled in him while the nausea died down. When he knew that he could hold it well enough, he capped the bottle and slung it on its strap beneath his shoulder again.

Then he got up on his feet and went on.

The North Star was up there, bright and clean among a billion other stars, shining hard against the charcoal-black sky. He held it out in front of him, while at the same time making sure to keep the Tortolitas on his right hand. They were over there a ways, not so far just now, a solid lump of dark against the shotgun scatter of stars that lay in back of them.

For a moment, while he took a bearing upon the Tortolitas, it occurred to him that he might be able to sneak around behind that foothill, climb it and run off with one of the Indian horses. It would save a heap of walking; and the horses, having passed the day with shade and water, would be good for some distance.

But in another moment he could see the foolishness of trying anything of that kind. Even to think of it was foolish, and it scared him. He'd have to keep on guard against thoughts that schemed to lead him away from developed plans. If he thought of anything, he would have to think safe thoughts, and not allow his mind to fool around with notions that could be dangerous.

Well, he could think about the money. That was safe enough to think of, and it was tied around his middle, the heavy weight reminding him of its meaning. Letting his fingers stray across the pockets woven in the webbing of the belt, he could feel the outlines of the coins through the canvas, solid and hard to the touch.

When you came down to it, he thought, they were the only thing worth thinking of right now, for they meant freedom for him from this crazy country. In any one of those pockets there was gold enough in double eagles to take him anywhere. Coming down to it, you could put almost everything in terms of gold, there being hardly a thing that gold would not do for a person nor hardly a place on earth it wouldn't take him.

And it was a good joke on Rodriguez, too—Rodriguez and his orders that a man should leave town. Well, he was; sure enough, he was, and it was a pity that Rodriguez couldn't enjoy his leaving.

That Rodriguez! For a space his mind drew up

to see him—squinty-eyed and greasy, and looking sidewise at him like he took him for a thief on first meeting! Running a rathole like the Apex with its sluts and filth and dirt floor, and sitting like a fat toad on gold enough to buy and sell the Territory.

By God, he'd had it coming, what he'd got.

He had, by God, and now his feeling flared up lively again. Just to think that some Mexican had had guts enough to tell him what to do, or not to do, made the blood pound up in his head. And it didn't matter, either, that he'd come out on the high end of it.

The thought was enough to make him see it happen again. He had never thought to see a Mexican lose his color; but even in the poor light of the small private room where Rodriguez kept his money and his accounts, he had turned as gray as a scrap of dirty linen.

The Mexican had had the sense of what was coming; that instant knowing of the truth that shows upon a man's face as sure as if he's been told. And before he'd seen the knife, too; for the knife was still in Jager's coat sleeve, where he often kept it hidden until the moment of its use. Rodriguez put his hand up, saying, "No! No!" but softly, as if begging, yet still knowing that it was of no use. When the blade went into his stomach you would think that he had died already in his mind and his heart.

But there'd be no more of him, and so it was a good joke, after all, and no matter that the thought of it still made him smart. But there'd be no more of him, nor of the Apex, nor of any place that bore a likeness to the Apex. Such days and places were over.

The thought of the different life that now lay open to him swelled in his mind and glowed there in radiant lights. From now on there would be crystal chandeliers hanging from chains above soft carpets, and the rooms would all be fixed in walnut and plush. He would play roulette in those surroundings; he would smoke the very best cigars, and drink the finest wines, and he would have a tailor make his clothing to measure. He would have the loveliest women hanging on his arm, maybe both arms. The women would be pink and soft, and they would bear themselves like queens and wear the latest styles in gowns and dresses. They would be willing when he wished them to be willing, too, and they would be too knowing to nag at his ways.

They'd not be common things like Maggie had always been.

Passing through his mind in that way, she held it for a moment so that he could feel her softness and her warmth, and that sense of willingness that seemed to drive up out of some deep place in her that needed filling. He could feel the burn again a little, too; but more easily than before, and only lingering for a space before she passed out of his mind.

Then the others had come back into it again, as smooth as pink piglets. To his ear there came the genteel whir of roulette wheels, and to his lips there came the dry tang of champagne served in long-stemmed glasses.

15.

The moon was up now, its light a soft sheen on the desert. It came up over the Tortolitas in a pulse of orange that paled to yellow as it climbed higher, and when it had a third of the sky beneath its reach, the color had gone white. Earlier, when he was still in good view of the Tortolitas, there was the chance of being made out by the Indians, if only by his movements. But that was back a number of hours, and there was no danger now.

Being hardly more than a quarter full, it wasn't much of a moon; and beyond the little frosty glowing of the sand, it didn't give much light. Here and there, behind a bush or large rock, a thin shadow might take form and spread out over the ground. Once its pale light was enough for him to see the motion of some small night thing that scuttled over his way.

He had bent his course some now. Instead of holding the North Star dead ahead, he held it off his right side, so that he quartered on it a little. Although he couldn't see it yet, he knew the broken splinter of the Picacho would be over that way. Bearing off to the left, more westerly, might bring him up a little shy of it, but there was still the road that lay off that way, and he would cut it if he strayed over too far. On the other hand, in holding hard to due north, the correction he might have to make when he was able to see the high, stony thumb could be a big one; and there was always the chance of passing it by in the dark, altogether.

Still, it was a safe move, going off to the northwest. And aside from that, it ought to shave some distance off the number of miles he had to go.

As he thought of that, the dead stage driver's estimate of twenty miles came into his mind. That would be from the far side of the pass, where the coach had paused before the climb had begun. Say there was a mile from there to the point in the pass where they were hit. Then say there was another mile beyond that to the wide curve where they had gone over.

That would make it eighteen from that point; and as the high rock on the outwash of the Tortolitas lay northeast of the wreckage, a line drawn from there to the Picacho might be less than eighteen miles. It could be seventeen, or even fifteen. The night was cooler, and he had a water supply. While not holding more than a quart, the bottle had been full, and it seemed a lakeful when he thought of how they'd gone all afternoon without a drop of any kind.

Anyway, whatever his chances might be, they looked better to him out here than back there at the rock with the others. Only an idiot would try to scale that slope to get the water in the tanks, there being no difference whether it was open day or in the dark hours. Muller had got exactly what he had coming to him. He deserved to get an arrow in him, and be damned to him.

Be damned to them all. Sitting around the bottom of that rock while every minute death crept closer was stupid business. Let them talk of somebody coming with help—they only wasted breath and built their hopes up for nothing. Come morning, they'd be singing a different song; or after the sun had worked a while longer on them . . .

All the same, he wondered if there was the chance of someone bringing help. It was hard to believe that Huston really thought there was, and yet it still could happen; and he knew that Huston's mention of that chance was one of the reasons that Jager set his mind to leave when he had.

Let someone come to find them, those who came would likely know about Rodriguez by now, and they would have him where they wanted him. He couldn't let that happen to him any more than he could stop and ask for help at the Picacho station when he got there. That was something else he'd have to work out. It was still a distance, but he'd need a good plan before he got there. Maybe he should lay out through the day—given he could stretch his water until dark; then with night he might be able to steal a horse and fill the water bottle at the station well. That would make him good enough for Pima country, anyway. But however he worked it out, he couldn't afford to be seen, or have it known that he'd gone by.

All night he walked across the desert, guiding on the North Star. Although he rested off and on, he tried to keep a steady pace to take advantage of the cool hours of darkness. He knew by this time that he'd never reach Picacho by sunrise, and that he'd have some travel left for day; so it was better that he push along as best he could while night favored him.

He would walk awhile; then he would lie down to rest, or simply sit. It was hard to tell how long he rested in those stops, not having a watch of any kind to tell him; but sometimes it would seem a long, long while, and then at other times it hardly seemed that a minute had passed.

In the longer-seeming times he would be scared, thinking he had gone to sleep, and he would jerk himself up onto his feet and start moving. In the shorter-seeming times, he could hardly order himself to rise, but he would do it, fearing that he was on the point of falling to sleep, and not daring to let it happen.

Off and on, when resting on the ground, he would count the seconds. He'd say aloud, "One, two, three," hearing his reedy voice in the darkness. It would help to keep his mind from drifting off, and help, too, to keep the threat of sleep at a distance. But then sooner or later, he'd lose himself among the numbers, and become confused, and would have to begin again. Still, it helped to keep him wakeful and alert.

While this did little to tell him how the time passed, the moon was helpful. Say it rose at eight, maybe a little later, the time would be close to midnight by now, if not beyond. It looked close to overhead, and all of the flimsy shadows had drawn in underneath the rocks and bushes.

Well, say it *was* midnight; that would be four hours. Then add a little for the time before the moon had come up; and if he made a mile an hour, that would be four, say five, miles that he could have made. Five from eighteen, say fifteen, left ten to go. Or had the moon risen later than eight? In summer, it was hardly dark then.

Well, it didn't really make much difference what it might be; he had to keep on going anyway, and the big thing was to keep his mind working. So long as it was occupied, and busy, it wouldn't wander off and fall asleep on him.

He watched the moon, seeing it like a great ship sailing west. Under the brush and rock, the shadows were beginning to put their edges out to the other side. Over in the south, he watched the fires in the cloud above the Catalinas. Then he watched that part of it that had brought the rain so near them, and had then moved off westerly. From the little he could tell by looking at the lightning throbbing in the cloud, it appeared to have divided from the main mass above the mountains. Maybe it was moving northerly a little, as well as westerly; he wondered if maybe the mountains to the west of him would get rain. There was no telling, either way, but it was a thing to keep the mind on, a thing to keep it wondering and guessing over. Right now that was the big thing; to keep his mind busy and working, and away from sleep.

But God Almighty, he was getting tired. It was different than in the afternoon when it had been the heat that wore and ground upon him. Now his legs seemed full of sand, and he could feel the tiredness hang upon him like a wet coat, pulling and dragging him down. A time or two, he caught his mind enjoying the thought of sleep, and he would jerk it away, as if it had been playing traitor to him. In the resting times, he had to be more careful; no more stretching out upon the earth the way his body yelled for him to do; now he had to sit upon the ground, and out away from any rock, so that he wouldn't be apt to lean upon it and drift off.

He watched the land, the massed cloud with its running lightning and far thunder, and the moon, so that he would stay wakeful. He began to wish that he had learned more of the desert so that he could think about the different plants and rocks and bushes by their names, instead of seeing them lumped together. Living in a town, you never cared much for that. Sitting at a gambling table all day, you didn't think about the desert too much. The game was enough.

There was still the moon to think of; and over some, the cloud mass that had broken from the bigger mass in the south. He was sure about that now. The moon was reaching over to the west more, and by its light it looked as if the new, separate cloud had come north still farther. He could see its deep fires, and now and then a fragment of its outline would be shown by lightning running and jabbing along its edges.

It would be raining there, he thought, above those far hills where the cloud was lying, and again he wondered if there wouldn't be a chance for the storm to move more toward him.

But while he hungered to have it rain upon him, and could almost feel the driving coolness on his dry skin, whether it did or didn't meant less to him just now than that he keep on wondering.

Just to wonder was enough for now. So long as he could do that, he would stay awake, and be able to move on.

So he watched the cloud, hardly daring to take his eyes away. It wasn't until a long while had passed that he realized he'd changed his course. All at once he knew it, and stopped moving. Fright took him—a fright so cold and mushy in his body that he nearly lost the strength to stand up. He stood as if he had been struck a blow and stared above him at the sky, trying to find the North Star in the black and brilliance of all the other stars that he saw.

Finally, it was there, just above him and a ways to his right; it was safe and sound, and he had only veered to the west a little. But even when it slowly grew upon him that he hadn't lost himself, after all, the cold and weakness of his fright worked in him still. After another moment, when he knew his legs would not work as they should, he let himself to the ground.

16.

When he looked again, putting his head up out of his arms, where it had gone of its own mind, the sky had changed. The light of the stars had lost its burning hardness, and many were gone from sight. The sooty deeps between the stars had turned the ashen gray of fires long burned out. The moon was still there. But it was far down in the west, and slipping into the bank of dark cloud.

It wasn't as it had been any more, either. It wasn't free and shining now, but dulled over and blotched, as if it had been cut from paper and pasted up on the sky. In the far east, a show of color lay across the earth. Against the clear, growing light, the pitch and fall of far mountains stood darkly sharp.

That was when he knew he'd fallen asleep. He was looking at the new day as it waited for the sun; and he knew the heat was waiting there, too.

"Sonofabitch," he said. It came out in a voice that sounded at a distance from him.

Then he said, "I'll be goddamned," but it came the same way. He said it again, "I'll be goddamned," and though he listened very carefully that time, it didn't change any. It was still the same, as though some other person had said it.

At first the notion startled him, so that he backed away from it, half wondering if someone had sneaked up on him while he was sleeping. Then it crept upon him and took hold of him, and made him turn his head about him slowly, and look on all sides.

But he was all alone, with no one else there.

My hearing's gone bad, he thought. Then he said it aloud, "My hearing's gone bad," and put his hands to his ears. He held them for a moment that way, pressing on them, and then he let go and listened again. But he couldn't tell much by that.

Then he wondered if it was his voice. Now that he remembered, it had sounded queer to him last night when he'd been counting whatever it was that he'd counted. With his voice box even drier now, it could easily be worse.

Then he ran his tongue out over his lips. They were stiff and broken, and the tongue came out upon them like a piece of thick, pebbly bacon rind. The size and foreign, leathery feel of it surprised him; but at the same time he felt better thinking that his throat had come to be the same way, than that his ears were no good.

Feeling easier in his mind, he got up onto his knees and took out the water bottle. He had himself a good drink, holding the water in his mouth a long while, and guarding well against the way his hands kept wanting to hold the bottle at his mouth. Then when he had capped it and hung it under his shoulder, he began to rise, getting his legs beneath him and pushing upward with his hands until his legs would bear all of his weight. Then, standing, he held himself with great care while he looked around and tried to make some sense of the swaying world.

Well, he had slept a time, but it was still there. Over behind him, the cloud above the Catalinas was now gone, raveled off to tatters. Back, too, but east more, the Tortolitas stood up clearly with the yellow strip of light behind them. Over in the west, the dark cloud that had got him into trouble had moved northerly again, so that it lay abreast of him now. It was closer, and lay black and swollen on the range of western ridges, as if it meant to tease him with what it held.

For a moment he wondered once more if there was a chance that it would come still closer and lay its cool rain on him. But that was what had got him into trouble in the first place. Had it not been for that cloud, he wouldn't have lost himself; nor would he have lost precious time in sleeping off the fit of weakness which the fright had given him.

To hell with you, he said to the cloud in his thoughts. Then he croaked it out loud. "To hell with you."

The high, broken thumb of the Picacho now stood out there a ways for him to look at, anyway. Seeming more of a smoky thought or notion than something real, it came up out of the dusk of early day some distance beyond him in the northwest. Only the peak was clear to see so early, with the shoulders and the steep flanks still held in haze and half-dark. It might be as much as eight or ten miles off, and it would be a good deal closer by this time if he hadn't slept. All the same though, it was good to see it out there; being sure of what you shot for was something.

Setting off, he held his eyes upon it. Even in the minute or so that he had looked for it and found it, it seemed to stand up more clearly in the lightening sky. But he watched it, even so. Now that he had found it, and was sure about his course again, he wasn't going to be teased away from it a second time.

He held a good pace for fifty yards or so, setting his feet down firmly while he guided on the far peak. Just to see it out there, and to know its meaning for him, gave him a kind of strength that, for a time, had the upper hand of his weariness.

But after a couple of minutes, the looseness started coming through his muscles. After going sixty or seventy yards, he felt his legs begin to wobble and give out. He felt the heaviness in him, the dead weight that dragged and pulled, trying to bear him down.

He saw a rock ahead, and when he came to it he sat upon its rough face to rest. Then, when he went on again, he thought to save his strength by going more slowly. But though it worked for a while, he felt the heaviness coming on him again soon enough.

First the legs went watery; then they wouldn't work the way he wished them to work; then the great weight bore him down.

There was no rock to sit on this time. Only the ground was there, and when he pushed himself up again, he ran so short of wind he had to stand there for a moment breathing in deep gasps. He might have been a lunger for the way his chest heaved and struggled at the air, yet hardly seeming to get enough. Nothing of that kind had ever happened to him before, and he tried to push the thought away to some other place; but it stayed to worry and nag him as he went on.

Then for a while he was more lucky. For the next stop, he had a ledge of granite to rest on; and beyond the ledge, he found a low rise of earth. Neither one had been a far walk, and he hadn't wearied too badly.

He was sitting on the low rise when he thought to lighten the load around his middle, and to sling it over his shoulders. Somewhere, he had heard that was the thing for long marches; and it did feel better having the gun belt and the money belt hung up higher. He understood that something queer had happened to his body, had maybe happened to it while he was sleeping; but it was good to think that he was learning to live with whatever it was.

The day was here now, the clear light was filling in the dim smoky places where dawn had come slower. In the foothills he could see the detail of the little ridges and draws, the beginning of color in them; though not yet the colors of the sun. But it would not be long now, for in the east, the sky was standing high in bands of yellow and red and orange.

When he stopped again it was a stop he hadn't planned on; but his body wasn't waiting on any plan this time. Of its own mind, a knee gave under him, then the other gave, too, letting him down. It didn't hurt him any, but he didn't like to think of what might have caused it. Resting there for a moment, he wondered at the ground he might have covered so far; but then he didn't like to think of that, either, and he didn't look around behind him to see. He wasn't so sure that he really wanted to know.

He went on for another forty yards or so, waiting to feel the warning that his knees would give him; but there was no warning that time at all.

He fell, straight down, his legs at all angles. He sprawled in a flat crash, hitting himself all over, his head in a glow of radiance.

That time he lay for quite a long while before he tried to move, and he knew now that something had gone badly wrong with his body. It was as if an enemy had slyly crept upon him and, unsuspected, worked its damage on him while he lay sleeping. It made him scary of himself, and while he lay there waiting for the radiance to pass he wondered at the ruin this enemy might have brought him.

Slowly, he got over on his butt and sat up. He made his hands go over his legs and body, feeling for injuries. His knees were skinned badly this time, and one of his cheeks had been bruised.

There was moisture under his finger tips and he could see the bloody redness on them when he took his hand from his face.

Then he saw another thing that made the sight of blood a small matter. Under the stain of red, the skin on his hand had turned a bluish color. Holding it out with the other before him, he stared at them together, and they were alike. Nor did putting them higher up into a better light make any difference. They were both blue, a faintly violet blue.

Blue! It almost left him in a shout. Of its own accord, his body lunged erect and his legs broke into a crazy gallop, as if it felt that it could leave those strange blue hands behind if only it hurried enough.

But they wouldn't be left behind him. No matter how his body ran, trying to get away from them, they still came. They were with it all the time, and hardly had the ground turned under him again and pitched him down upon it than his hands were wrenching at the bottle of water under his shoulder, tearing away the cap and ramming it up to his mouth where his tongue and throat, suddenly now in league with his treacherous hands, pulled and sucked upon the bottle until the water was gone.

Then they let it fall; and as innocent as lambs, came down to either side of his legs, where they lay quiet.

"So," he said. He took a breath, and let it out and looked at each hand in turn. "So," he said again. "So that's how it's going to be."

He understood about them now. He got up on his knees where he could see them better, and looked at them again. They had been his good friends all of his life; now they did this to him. Now that he needed them so badly, they went against him; and not only that, either, but they schemed with other parts of his body, turning the whole thing to his downfall: legs, arms, throat, lungs, everything. Even his ears.

But now he understood about the changes in his body. Being aware of all their sly ways, he knew things would be different. He felt calm and in command, thinking how he understood their ways and how he would deal with them. Within his head, his thoughts about them stood out cold and clear in large pictures. If it was a fight his body wanted, he was ready for a fight.

Staying on his knees a moment longer, he took the heavy gun belt, together with the knife that he had hung on it earlier, off his shoulder, and let it fall. More than needing them for anything that might be ahead, he needed freedom from their weight. He took his coat off, too, and let that fall; then he slung the empty bottle around his neck against the time when he would find a place to fill it. Now, with the money belt in place around his shoulder, he was ready to go on again.

That time he made ten yards before he fell. He got up and went ahead and made another fifteen yards before he fell again. This time, instead of rising right away, he made a plan. He crawled a ways in order to throw his body off the scent of his designs. After he thought it might be confused enough, he got to his feet and walked. He was able to make almost two dozen steps before his legs caught on to this deceit.

Together with the ground he'd covered in the crawl, it wasn't too bad. Added up, it came close to twenty yards, altogether; a little less maybe. If he was careful not to use the plan too much, he could beat this sly, conniving body of his yet.

That time when he fell, he landed near a wash that crossed the plain from the west. Crawling over the last few yards, he lay beside it while he looked down into it to find the easiest way to cross over. It was deep, seven or eight feet, on the average. The high banks pitched sharply upward, rising in a straight cut from the bottom. It seemed to head up in the hills beneath the cloud, and wind off over the plain to the eastward, turning and snaking along. The bottom of the wash was largely bare of growth, something that he thought strange, drawing on the little that he knew of washes; ordinarily they had a little vegetation in them.

But that wasn't the problem, anyway, and it was hard to think of more than one thing at a time. He lay there on the edge for several moments trying to find the best way to cross over. Then he got up on his knees in order to see along the banks on either side of where he was lying. There seemed to be no easy slope near him, however; and after searching for as far as he could see clearly to the east and west, he came closer to the edge and leaned out to get a better look at the bottom.

That was when the money belt came free, slipping off of his shoulder and down his arm, falling in a dead weight. He reached, grabbed and missed, and nearly fell, himself, over the edge. The belt dropped in a heavily turning circle, and when it struck, the weight of the gold coins burst through onto the sand from some of the pockets.

"Shit!" he said. Then he thought, well, hell, what difference did it make? He had to cross over someplace, and he could search along this thing all day long and likely find it all alike. He might as well try finding a breakdown in the bank along this stretch of the wash as anywhere. He had to go down there anyway, now.

He would like to rest a while longer, but at that moment all of the coins that had burst out and lay there yellow and dull in the sand turned bright to the eye. In the bottom of the wash, the pale gray sand went white, and little knots of black shadow stood out behind the few stones. Everything around him had taken on a sharpened line, and when he turned his head to look east, he saw the sun come edging up over the rim of the world.

The sun was quite enough to make him move. Bellied down again, he swung one leg out over the emptiness below, then the other. Gripping the edge with his elbows, he started letting down, but as it now bore all of his weight, the earth began to crumble and then a part of it broke loose and one elbow shot through. The sudden shift of weight worked upon him, turning his body sideways in the air; and though he kicked in order to right himself, he hadn't the time before he came down.

He fell in a flat, broad slam, the breath in him become a vacuum. His head roared and filled with bright lights again. Little gravel, fragments of the hard caliche, and streams of sand poured over him while he lay there on the bottom clutching for air.

Maybe a minute passed before he got it coming into him well enough to move. Then he made himself get over on his stomach. His body would like to lie there for the rest of the day, but whether it wished to or not, it would have to move. Already, the sun was getting strong in the bottom, and he was afraid of what would happen to him if he wasted time. Another hour, maybe less than an hour, it would be a furnace down there.

When he got to his knees, he crossed the few remaining feet of sand to the belt. The coins were flung around it in a circle in the white sand. First, he reached out for the belt, and picked it up to fasten it around his middle; but he forgot about the pockets, and when he raised it up, more of the coins spilled out of those that had opened.

When that happened, he set it down before him on the sand carefully. Then he spread it out, and when he had it good and flat, he buttoned all of the pockets. Then he lifted it again, slung it around his middle, and buckled the belt in front. He was all done taking chances with it over his shoulder, weight or not.

Now he let himself rest for a moment. The thought and effort required and spent to work that all out had left him panting and tired. Breathing was still a labor in his chest, and the roaring had stayed on in his head and would not leave.

He wouldn't allow himself to rest beyond a minute, however; or what he took as a minute. Then he reached out and began to gather the coins in to him. When he had a number of them in his hand, he opened one of the web pockets in the front of the belt and slipped them into it. After he had filled another one, he tried to put some into a pocket back under his arm; but here he had trouble. In some way his fingers had become stiff and couldn't open the button.

He laid the coins in front of him and put his hands to his face. Now he was trying to think it all out clearly and quietly. It was such a simple

202

thing. He had filled the pockets of the belt before, and so easily; what was wrong now? If only he knew what the trouble was. If only he could think. If only the roaring would leave his head. He moved his hands to his ears, trying to make it leave; but it would not leave. If anything, it was somewhat louder.

He stared at the coins on the sand and now he put his whole mind on the problem. He carefully took the belt off and laid it on the smoothest part of the sand, tilting it so that the pockets would not spill any more coins out. Then he opened the pocket that had troubled him before, and filled it. When he had that buttoned down securely, he opened up another.

He was just beginning to fill it when the roaring in his ears became louder. It was really much louder, and he paused, holding the coins in his hands, and listened. It came a whole lot louder than before, and it made him wonder that his ears could make a sound of that kind. Maybe they could, but what about the way the earth was shaking?

The shaking made him feel uneasy and he felt over his body with his hands, but it wasn't shaking. Then he looked around him at the sides of the wash. However, there was nothing there to tell him anything. The banks went reaching up too high above for him to see what might lie beyond. Overhead he could see a part of the cloud which he had followed. As it now seemed to be much closer than it had earlier, he wondered if the shaking and the sound could be thunder.

He began to rise, trying to see the cloud better. He felt the shaking now become a deep pounding slam, and then as he stood up and looked there came to be an odd kind of motion in the wash. It was something like a hundred yards away, near the turning of a bend, but at first it told little of itself.

He was standing now and staring, squinting in the glare of hard light. This was nothing of a kind that he had ever seen before, and he could feel a fright begin to grow in him now. Then the fright grew bigger until it seemed to match the speed with which the strange motion came. It was vast, too, this motion; and for all of his staring at it he could only think that it was made of what the wash was made of—and it came on, tawny, heaving, fluid in its forward rush.

Then he knew, and the knowing filled him like a revelation.

"No!" It came in a scream, the whole of his body knowing and screaming. "No!" Terror tore up through his body, the knowledge burning in his head like the light of the sun.

"No!" he screamed again, and he could see it all now very well. The wash was filled with run-off from the hills that lay to the west; stone, snags of brush, whole uprooted trees, a mortar of churned mud and raw earth convulsed and beaten in a foam of downward-bearing waters from the cloud.

He turned, running for the bank in one motion. He leaped in a wild spring, reaching while his hands clawed at the edge above and missed. He fell upon the coins and belt, reached down, seized the belt, stumbled to his feet, and lunged again for the bank.

Then everything seemed to move more slowly. He saw his feet move out and rise as if he moved them at a slow walk. He was able to see his hands reach slowly up, and it surprised him that the ends of all of his fingers should be covered with blood. He saw the earth break down under them, and when he fell again his feet dropped into flowing water.

The coins sprang high in the air, their golden faces fired by the bright sunlight. He caught their brilliance in his eye, and held them in it as the last thing on earth he saw before the torrent bore him down under.

He felt himself submerged, borne aloft to dim light, then turned below to darkness, and smashed. And it was a crime, he thought—while life still beat in him enough to have a thought of any kind. It was the crime of all crimes, the greatest outrage of them all.

Who in the name of God would ever think that, out here in this thirsting desolation, he could drown?

17.

The false dawn seemed to Patterson as if the sun would rise in the west, for at his back the Tortolitas blocked his view to the east and the first sign of color appeared upon the peaks and ridges to the west.

Patterson was lying down behind a small Spanish dagger plant. It grew up out of the foothill about a quarter of the distance to the trees from the bottom. It was well above the level of the plain, and nearly even with the top of the high rock, a number of yards off. It was small, only a foot or two high, but it gave the only cover he could find in all that stretch of bare ground.

However, there were virtues. While there was nothing better in sight, the isolation gave him a degree of privacy in which to think, and he could see out a great distance. The view gave out on the plain and on all of the blistering ground that they had crossed yesterday. He could see the ragged, raw ranges in the west; he saw the splintery, bare thumb of the Picacho, and he saw the low cloud mass that they had watched last evening with such yearning, and that now lay darkly on the line of hills across the wide plain, somewhat to the northwest of them.

About all that he didn't have a view of was

the others, who were down below him hidden by the high rock. Rather than look upon that as an inconvenience, however, it appealed to him. Having them out of sight had given him the only chance he'd had in which to think clearly. The way they watched him, trying to guess if he had any plans, got on his nerves.

He had been there for two or three hours before the sky began to gray over. At that time there had seemed to be a chance of sneaking through the darkness to the tanks and taking the Indians by surprise. Then it had occurred to him that he wouldn't see all three of them in time, and that dawn might bring him a better opportunity. So he had settled down behind this dagger plant to wait for dawn; but now that it had come, he still waited.

He hitched himself to a better position on the rough ground. He was careful of the sharp stones, and of the dagger plant. In the darkness, he had speared himself a few times on the vicious blades, and the cuts still hurt him.

It was a cruel and barbarous thing, that dagger plant, or Spanish bayonet, as he had heard it called. It seemed so unnecessary, too, so that he wondered why the good Lord had ever made a thing of that kind. But everything was like that out in this country—a barbarous, bitter land that shocked a man's mind and warred against his body. You would almost think that God had planned it as the slag heap of the world, and had made of it a dumping ground for all the shavings and the filings and the cinders that He had left over when He'd finished off the fairer parts. That's exactly what it was, a slag heap; and a human being had no business being in it at all.

Never had Patterson seen a land that was so barren of any promise, or so hostile in aspect. Not even in imagining what his crossing of the country might reveal, had he had a vision of such appalling qualities. It made no difference that he had a fair amount of knowledge of these western reaches, gleaned from tales his father had told him of the war fought with Mexico.

But nothing he had heard his father tell of came up to this. He had been prepared for rude companions and a rigorous journey through the raw wilderness. He had not been ready to die of thirst, nor perish at the hands of naked savages. And these people he was with. Where on earth did such people come from?

What kind of man could Jager be to openly beat a woman? To knock her down and then run off with water that he had hidden from the rest of them, the only water they had? And what about the woman who would associate with such a man as Jager? But it was easy enough to guess about her, bedizened and painted as she was, or as she had been.

And Huston. The doctor who performed his

surgery with a pocket knife. He looked to be a man of some education.

Then there was Muller who, though no more than a boy, had still been a soldier. But he had been a deserter, and saying that, you had said all there was to say about one who would violate a sacred trust. That's what military service was.

Neither was there very much to say for Wagner, though the reasons were different. But it was plain enough that Wagner was an old man who ought to be at home with his carpet slippers and pipe, rather than be out here chasing young dreams of gold.

And he had asked for all this, too—chosen of his free will to cross the land by stagecoach, thinking it his duty to see this frontier of his country with his own eyes—rather than take advantage of an easy sailing passage around the bottom of South America.

That was where the irony lay. It was something he had asked for. It showed you what could happen when you let yourself be carried away by a patriotic impulse.

He hitched again; he took a sharp stone from under him, and then looked a long while above him at the trees upon the stone outcrop. This might be the time to try it, he thought. This might be the time. If only the Academy had taught a course in this kind of fighting, he could be certain. Or if he had read it in a book at one time, and had seen it plotted in stages of maneuver on tactics charts, he would not have this indecision. No book had ever told him how it could be done.

But he could not sit forever behind this dagger plant, for now across the plain the sun began to touch upon the mountains and the low, wrinkled hills. The peak of the Picacho stood up like a candle flame. A tongue of running fire went licking at the broken spines of ranges that, a moment ago, were soft silhouettes. Could he forget the implications of that light, the view could be a study in a rare, exotic beauty; but when time was running out, they would not be forgotten.

The sunlight shone upon the far cloud now, too. He could see the shading of its dark, rounded convolutions, and how the rain fell from it toward the hills underneath. In the sky, the heavy, opaque streams were glinting in the light of the sun.

But how devilish it was! How devilish that cloud was to let its rain down there where it could not help them; flaunting it, you might even say; wasting the bounty of its waters in that cruel, heedless manner. But it was like everything else in this impossible country. All of it was cruel and heedless.

Perhaps, he thought, the rain fell on Jager, and that would help him reach the station at Picacho, and that in turn would help the group here at Tinajas Altas.

For a moment Patterson imagined that he *had* got that far, and in his mind he could see him. He would stand there, Jager would, beneath the black, swelling cloud, with the rain descending on him. His face would turn upward, and he would be laughing as the downward-falling waters soaked into him. On the ground, little puddles would be forming, and he would drink from them and from them he would fill the water bottle.

He could almost feel the cooling freshness on his own body; and then he felt his neck swell at the thought that such a man as Jager should enjoy so much luxury. Still and all, there was nothing to do but wish him well.

He turned his back upon all across the plain and looked upward once more through the long blades of the Spanish dagger plant. He was lying flatter now, for even in those short moments that he had looked off, the light had grown. By now, the mesquite trees above the tanks were definitely green. Underneath them, the rock and stone block that shaped the edges of the tanks began to have form. He began to see the slot from which the arrow had come streaking at Muller yesterday.

There was light enough now to see himself, too. Looking at his legs, he could make out the slashings that he had cut for ventilation in his trousers. He could see his boots, too, or what remained of them now, for they were little more than sandals, or those huaraches that he had seen along the way, that Mexicans wore.

He felt a definite pain to think of what his uniform had cost him, and hardly a month back. But more than money lost, he felt his being reduced to rags and tatters a brutal assault upon his sense of "military presence."

"Military presence" was a thing that he had heard of from his earliest years; a concept of his father's meant to embody and express the finest attributes a soldier might have. His childhood had been filled with talk of it, for it was woven through that vast catalogue of tales that his father told of going down to Mexico with General Scott, back in 1847.

According to his father, who liked nothing better than to reminisce upon those gallant, dead days, General Winfield Scott had been perfection in uniform. It was hard to describe the honor one felt in being appointed to his staff, to be the envy of many another officer not so fortunate as to receive this accolade. General Scott was widely known throughout the Army for his commanding mien, for his impeccable attire, and for that sense of nicety that he had—a properness that went even so far as to embrace the very conduct of his campaigns. There was certainly little question but that Scott had been a general in the old classic mold. Or that he had been the living spirit of all those special qualities embodied in "military presence."

That was how his father spoke of him, and Patterson had never questioned what his father said about the Army. But, granted Scott had taken certain airs on himself, they still befitted him; and they hardly warranted that cruel, shameful nickname that his troops had seen fit to give him. Old "Fuss and Feathers," they called him; and how ridiculous, how unmilitary, how undignified it was! But even in its absurdity, it nevertheless suggested more propriety and seemliness than did "Rough and Ready," the curious name that public adulation had bestowed upon General Zachary Taylor after his defeat of Santa Ana at Buena Vista. His father always puzzled over that.

Not that Patterson's father would have it felt that he thought little of Taylor's valor. Quite the contrary, in fact. Nothing could be farther from the truth. It was simply that he didn't feel that Taylor measured up to Scott's stature. And nothing better pictured Taylor's lack in that particular regard than his casual attitude toward military history, his bland dismissal of traditional Army methods; or, by God, his going into battle in a linen duster, riding on an old yellow mule. And of his whole long catalogue of faults, the linen duster and the old yellow mule were somehow the worst.

But there you had it. And there you had the

essence of "military presence," too. Whether it was good or bad, or whether it was right or wrong, it was related in his mind to all that he had ever learned about the Army and soldiering. The loss of it divested him, and this entire situation, of any dignity, and reduced it to the same level as guerrilla fighting. He was glad his father could not see him just now.

It was quite light now, and Patterson could see the barren, rough slope clearly. The large stone slabs that formed the tanks were separate from one another. The trees possessed a depth; those in front were lighter in their shading than those farther back. The darkness that remained was more of a natural shadow and shade. And, except in full sunlight, it would not get much lighter up there than it now was.

There would not be any question now about his being able to see the Indians, once he got in among them; or about the view that they would have of him, while he was on his way up there. If he was going to go, he would have to go soon. Given another few minutes, the last remaining dullness of the slope would be gone, and then whatever move he made would surely be seen at once. Then they had only to pin him down.

He lay there, looking through the long dagger blades, out along the rising pitch of the slope above him. He moved his hand ahead, the one that held his revolver. He looked at the revolver, checking it again and wondering if he ought to change the charges once more. In lying there from dark to daylight, he had already changed them once, and the primers twice. Still, another change, all around this time, would do no harm.

But then he knew he was just begging time, and there was no more for him to beg. You couldn't hold the sun back.

He began to gather himself, moving his legs to get his knees under his body. Then when he was resting that way, resting on his elbows and knees against the stony earth, he looked again through the blades of the dagger plant.

It had changed again, but now the change was different, and not a matter of mere shadow and light. It was something that he saw, or thought he saw. Just as he had seen him in the flesh yesterday, he now saw Muller going up that slope again. He could see him running in the white light with his revolver waving. He could see the arrow coming, and how Muller turned on one foot as the arrow struck and turned him in a part of a circle. He could almost feel it going into himself.

It was going to be that way again; he knew it was, as strongly as though it came to him as revealed truth. It was going to happen to him in that exact manner, just as it had happened to Muller; and all at once he saw the barrel of his revolver shaking. He put his free hand to his eyes, but in his mind the gun went on shaking just the same. Inside of his mind, a voice kept crying out to stop, for God's sake, stop! But that made no difference, and the barrel still shook.

The voice cried out in his mind again to stop, and then he heard a new kind of voice. He heard it, too, not in his mind. It came from some distance, and it seemed to be a woman's voice calling his name. He put his head up, then he took his hand away from his eyes and listened, and it came again.

"Lieutenant?" It was clearer now, and came from the hidden side of the high rock. "Can you hear me? Are you anywhere near?"

There was no mistake about it, he was being called by Miss Hale. He wanted to shout out, "Yes! Yes! I'm here!" but that would be too dangerous; with any luck the Indians could reach him from above with their arrows. When she called again, asking did he hear her, and would he come to them, he began to slide down.

Moving away from the dagger plant, he could feel that he was shaking more than ever; but he did not mind that now. He felt the way a man must feel when he has been reprieved upon the moment of execution. And whatever he might have thought about Miss Hale before, he knew that in this moment he was intensely grateful to her.

18.

He came on slowly past the rock where they had all been sitting or lying since first they had come here. The girl had come to the point, around the shoulder, to call him, and was leaning on it, resting herself, as he came on. What had been a fine gown now was stiff with blood and salt and Muller's vomit; it was torn, too, in places, and badly wrinkled, and she wore it with an air that made it seem as if the night had aged her by a dozen years. But his sense of gratitude was too strongly felt for him to be critical of her.

Her hand moved when he came in sight of her and a tired smile began to lift at her mouth.

"Did you call?" he said when he was nearer. "I heard someone call."

She nodded while she pushed her weight away from the rock.

"Yes, I called. I didn't know if you heard or not. I guess you did though."

"Yes," he said, "I heard. Anything wrong?"

And then he marveled that he could speak so. It seemed to imply that he had come to some acceptance of their situation as a normal state of affairs, and that only some sensational thing could qualify as being "wrong."

But she didn't seem to think he'd said anything queer.

"No," she said. "I guess we're doing the best we can. We're all still alive, anyway. The sun will be along though, and we want to move around to the other side of the rock."

Nothing much had changed from last evening, or in the early morning hours when he had left them and had gone up the slope to lie behind the dagger plant. Except for Miss Hale, nobody else appeared to have moved, and all were lying as when he saw them last. The old man was now awake, although his eyes were glazed, which made it hard to tell if he was really conscious. Muller lay in a flush of fever, while his breathing sounded quick and shallow; but the bloodstains on his bindings were dark now and old. There was also blood, fresher blood, upon the rag that Huston wore around his head to cover the cut from Jager's gun.

But nothing had really changed. They were lying as they had been lying now for twelve hours, still hanging on.

Huston's eyes were closed, but they opened when Patterson neared.

"Ah, the troops," he said. He got over on his stomach and began to rise. He stood up all the way, swaying and reaching for balance. "The day is saved, now the troops are here. How's the strategy today?"

Patterson could feel his face becoming redder than it already was. It was back to this again, but it was nothing you could sensibly argue with civilians. Only another soldier could appreciate the impossibility of that slope. And not a deserter, either.

"Miss Hale called to say you wished to move," he said, and he stood up very straight in all his rags to make it clear that strategy was not in Huston's province.

But Huston didn't seem to notice the correction. Nor did he seem devoted any longer to the theme of strategy.

"Yes," he said, and then he stopped. Then he made a new beginning. "Yes, we'll have to move." He swayed more, and his hands raised to his head. "God, that was a lick. No, we can't stay here much longer."

"All right, we'll get over beyond the rock. It ought to do all right until noon."

"Noon?" Huston said, letting his hands come down. He stared around him while he steadied on his feet. "Yes, noon. . . . Well, we'd better get on with it. I'll take his feet. You can help Miss Hale along with the rest of him."

"All right," Patterson said, "that's good enough, I guess."

"Well, we might as well get on with it," Huston said.

Huston seemed fairly steady by now, looking

down at Muller and planning how they should carry him. But Patterson could not get out of his mind how he had said "noon"—how the word had sounded. It might have been the name of some exotic land.

They carried Muller first; Huston had his legs and Patterson and Miss Hale took hold of him beneath his shoulders and around his body. They went slowly over the ground, but Muller had that peculiar, shifting weight of dead or sleeping persons, and the going was awkward. The load and the rough ground made it necessary to watch their footing carefully; but Patterson found it better than watching Muller. Now that he had failed to make an effort to reach the water, it was harder to look at Muller than it had been earlier.

When they found a place beneath the western face of the rock, where the morning shadow would fall, they set Muller down. As Huston had been staggering badly on the way, he lay with Muller on the ground while Patterson and the girl returned to get Wagner. He was hard to raise up, but once they had him moving with his arms across their shoulders, he went along well enough.

Still and all, the sum of two men was a load, and Patterson became aware of the drain upon his strength. Sitting against the rock, he felt a numbness in his arms and legs, and he could hear the beat of his heart up in his ears. His hands were trembling with the great exertion and his lungs pumped and strained.

It was hard to believe that the simple act of helping two men over ten yards of ground could leave you bordering on collapse; but perhaps it wasn't all that. Perhaps he had been failing all the time, and until this showed it up, had not known it.

He had been worried over how he looked before, but he now began to think of how he was feeling. He wasn't used to having his body going back on him in this way. Physical condition was a thing the Academy prized.

Nobody had the breath or will to speak for some time. Patterson looked out over the wide plain, watching the sunlight creeping toward them from the far distance. It now shone full upon the western mountains, and was steadily backing over the level ground, as, behind them, it reached farther above the Tortolitas into the sky. It was like an enemy advancing, he thought; slowly and relentlessly and unopposable, it came on. Soon it would define the shadow of the rock which reached over them; then it would begin to eat upon the perimeter of the shadow; and the rock, after the pattern of its ageless warfare with the desert sun, would shorten up its defenses, as if believing that the timeless and eventual outcome might in some way be changed.

But it couldn't, of course; it could never be changed in any way. Soon enough, the sunlight would absorb the dark shadow, and with the shadow it would have them. That would be at noon, very likely, and while the afternoon would see the rock restore itself and change the tide of battle, those few hours when the sun held all of its horrors overhead could easily be enough to make the shadows, that would later grow in the afternoon, of no meaning to them. He was beginning to see what the word "noon" had meant for Huston.

After a long while Muller stirred on the ground. He moved a hand, and then his eyes opened. They held upon the sky over his head, glassy and blank, and when he spoke his voice had something of a blankness, too.

"Water," and after the one word his eyes closed again.

The girl put out her hand and laid it on his forehead. Huston touched Muller's wrist. The others glanced at Muller, but no one else spoke. There was only the dry, blank sound of Muller's one word among them.

After a moment went by, it came again, the dry, blank word.

"Water."

"There'll be water soon," the girl said this time. She bent her head over his face, and her eyes came up to Patterson when she straightened again.

Patterson looked away. He felt uneasy looking at Muller now that he was lying in that way. Had Muller not gone running up the slope as he had, Patterson could look upon him easily. And it made no difference that he told himself that Muller had been out of his head.

"Water," Muller said again.

"His fever's up again," Huston said. He put his hand on Muller's neck, under the jaw. "Yes, it's up."

Patterson, from the tail of his eye, could see that Muller's face was shiny and quite red. He kept staring at the cloud across the wide, brilliant plain. He wished to God, as he had never wished for anything before, that rain would come across to where they were.

"Maybe the rain will come," he said, though not meaning to. It was as if the thought turned of its own will into spoken words.

Then, having said it, he turned and looked at Huston; but Huston shook his head.

"Not by day," he said. "Not that one. The airs are all wrong. It can't last, anyway."

"There's Jager, then. He ought to make Picacho soon. He's been on his way all night, nearly ten hours now."

But Huston shook his head over Jager, too.

"He only had a quart of water," he said. Then he paused turning his head and looked at Miss Hale, so that it seemed he had been holding something back and now wondered how it would strike her.

But when he said. "I doubt he got much more than halfway," she only moved her head slowly, so that you thought that she had settled her mind on Jager before he went off and left them.

"Didn't you say we had a chance of being found out here?" Patterson said.

"Yes," Huston said. "Yes, I expect we will be." He looked down at Muller, and then up again. "Eventually."

Patterson looked away again across the desert. Huston was against him all the way now. It was all the same to Huston: Jager getting through to find help for them, the cloud that might have come here with rain, the chance of being found by searchers. None of it made any difference to him.

"Water," he heard Muller say, and he could feel the eyes of Miss Hale on his face. He knew she was against him, too.

"Water," Muller said again. He kept on saying it—the voice far away and dusty in sound, while they all listened. Then they looked at Patterson all together, as if to show how they agreed among themselves in being against him.

Patterson reached and pulled himself with his hands along the rock until he stood up. He was sick and tired of having them watch him, and thinking of him as they thought. He wanted room around himself, and he wanted to be away from where they were. Thinking of it again, he could better have kept quiet when Miss Hale came out to call him, and not answered her. At least, if he had stayed up there beneath the dagger plant, he wouldn't now be bothered by hearing Muller, or by looking at him; no more than by the way the others talked, or how they looked at him, either; their thoughts being easily as plain as what they might say.

So he stood up and pushed himself along the rock; he moved around the shoulder toward the point, and as he came around it to the far side the sun struck at him in a blast of such power that it made him lean against the rock to hold himself upright. Then he jerked his hands away and stumbled back; already the sun was in the stone surface and the heat was like a stove lid.

He drew off more and made his way ahead to where more rock stood up between him and the others. Now that he was over here, hidden somewhat, he thought to water out—and failed painfully.

He went slowly back around the rock again, feeling the bigness of the scare in him. It made him wary of himself, so that he noticed other things, too—the way his feet stalled when they bumped against small stones; how, for no apparent reason, his knees kept wanting to buckle—and together with the pain of trying to urinate, they made him wonder what had happened to his body.

All at once, he'd come to have the infirmities of a failing old man.

He sat again, but at a distance from the others this time. The scare had put a loneliness upon him, but he didn't want to be with them yet.

The desert was full of sunlight by now, and the shadow of the high rock was beginning to draw inward a little. Even at this early hour the air above the surface shook with waves of heat. He could see the mountains quiver in a soft, liquid motion, seeming to hang in mid-air. From the far cloud, rain had stopped falling now, and there had even come to be a lightening of its heavy dark color. A part of it, with fluffy white edges, was separating from the larger mass; blue showed through the widening gap.

The breakup of the far cloud made the loneliness weigh on him still more heavily. He could see a part of the slope from where he sat, too. If only they could understand about it, he thought. If only they could understand about that slope, and see it from a military viewpoint, as he saw it himself. Then they wouldn't watch him as they did, and think the things about him they did, just because he wore a uniform, and because Muller had tried to get up there yesterday. That alone should be enough to tell them how futile it would be for him to try it now.

If only he had a squad, he thought, it would be the easiest thing in the world and he would have the water in a matter of minutes. But he hadn't, and going up there alone would end in sure death.

That was what he wished they could understand. If they could only see it in that way, they surely wouldn't feel toward him as they did, nor would he have this loneliness on him. He was aware of feeling kindly and forgiving toward them all at once, and he would like to go to them and take them by the hand, each in his turn— even Muller—and explain it to them. But, of course, he couldn't do that; not when the feeling toward him ran as it did. Just the same it was enough to make him go back in his mind over the long time they had been at this place, in order to see if there was anything he had missed.

For all that time had come to be a very strange thing by now. Events still seemed to be clear enough. In his mind, he saw it all, beginning with the wreck and with Wagner leading them across the desert toward these hills. Then the big letdown of finding Indians in possession of the water; the waiting in the deadening heat while trying to think it all out, until Muller had gone yelling up there.

He could see it all, just as it had happened, and real enough to make it seem that it was all happening again.

He could see what happened later: how Huston and the girl had got the arrow out of Muller; and how it seemed that Muller was a special person who had for them a certain meaning that denied the fact of his desertion. It had been most apparent when Huston had lashed out at him, defending Muller, saying that at least he'd made a try to get the water. Having Huston turn upon him remained the clearest in his mind.

But he could see the night in his mind, too, the forming of the clouds above the Catalinas, how they came near, but not quite near enough, and how the rain which fell did so far off, and was of no help. And Jager going crazy and running off with the water.

Then he saw them as they now were, waiting while the sun ate through the shadow toward them and wondering what the end would be like. Or knowing what would happen, what the end would be, and simply waiting for it to come; for it came, at long last, down to that, and it had to be admitted.

Maybe they were lucky getting this far, and lasting to this point. If Wagner had been wrong, they would not have had any hope at all, and so he could be thanked for that much, at least. You couldn't live on hope for too long, but it could keep you going for a while, anyway.

Except for Huston's quick fingers, Muller would have gone off in a matter of minutes of being hit. And save for Miss Hale's sitting with him through the long night while Huston was too dazed to help him any, Muller might have died then. But he hadn't. And the girl had pulled him through the dark hours. Simply talking to a person, letting him know that you were near by and watchful, was helpful to him.

He seemed to see them all from some distance, and it came over him, as he looked upon it in that manner, that all of them had helped in some way to keep them going. You could even say that Muller had—no matter what his reasons had been. He had tried, as Huston said. Even Jager, if he reached a settlement, would have helped them, however dark his motives had been.

All at once then, that brought it down to himself; and that was when he knew that, of them all, he stood alone in having done nothing. He hadn't helped in any way whatever.

All that he really had done was stall for time and raise objections. He'd laid up under the dagger plant and tried to raise comparisons between this situation and those classic models of his days at the Academy. That it didn't conform with them had made him raise a smoke screen to shield his doubts and inexperience and his inability to face up to it. He'd talked a lot of theory that did not apply to what they had here, and how things could be, but were not. He had damned the country, but damning it made no difference.

All the while that life was ebbing out of them, he'd thought of troops and how he would do this or that, had he had them. In this particular moment, in this particular piece of the United States, he was all there was to the Army. Now if he failed them they'd be on his conscience for so long as he might live. There was still more. There was young Muller. Whatever had driven him up that slope, Muller had taken his chances and had made the effort to climb it. It didn't work any longer that he tell himself that Muller had been out of his head, or had a hangover from drinking on the coach. He had gone. Nor did it work that he look down upon Muller for deserting. If anything, the knowledge that a man who would desert would dare to go where he himself had not been able to go, made it worse.

He knew he couldn't have a thing of that kind hanging over him. He hadn't been raised to abide a feeling of disgrace with comfort. At least that little of his sense of "military presence" was left to him.

That was when he knew he really had no choice about the proper thing to do. No matter how it turned out, he had to make a try to reach the water alone.

He got again to his feet and slowly worked around the point of the rock, to the far side. He had left his tunic there when they'd moved, and now he meant to put it back on. If he was going to get killed, it would be according to regulation, and with what measure of dignity he could muster.

The hill was now there in the white torch of sunlight, and he scanned the broad, open slope while he worked the buttons through the slits in the blue cloth. Then, when he had finished, he took his pistol from the scabbard at his belt and changed the primers. Now he began to wonder if he should go around and tell the others his plans; to let them see for themselves that he wasn't the coward they might have thought. That was the word that came to his mind.

But in the next thought, he set his mind against it. They would know it soon enough in any event, however it might turn out. It would only smack of false heroics anyway, and serve to let them think that he had been moved to do it by what they might think of him. It wouldn't do to let them have ideas of that kind; after all, they were still civilians.

Still, he felt a friendliness and warmth for those people, and in the way of one who goes away toward something, the end of which is unknown in advance, and sees the persons and the places he has known go dim to his sight, he wished them all well. It even crossed his mind to intercede in some way or other in behalf of Muller, when the time should come for him to write up his report of this business—if such a time should ever come.

He stood ready now. His forage cap sat squarely on his head, the bill low. His tunic was buttoned up to his neck, and the sweat was beginning to flow down inside. His revolver was in his right hand, the charges sure in the chambers and the primers fresh. He would never be more ready than he now was, and as he had his mind settled, the time had come.

So he started, moving slowly up the slope. He took his time in order to save the little strength he had so that he would be steady when the range was right. He put the hand that held the revolver out before him, ready to fire, and as the slope began to bear him above the plain, he held his arm to suit the level of the pitch, as though he had been shooting at the bull ring on the range, back at the Point. Looking through the sight groove, he could see the front blade on the cleft between the large stones through which Muller had been hit; and he held the blade there because it seemed the only place where they could get a look at him without exposing more of themselves than was safe. The slot was fairly small, but he had made a marksman's rating at the Academy; if he was steady enough, and had the time, he might do some good. The Point might not be a total loss, after all.

He was higher now, and in the wide, reaching openness he felt naked and stripped. He had covered nearly half the ground to be crossed, and was in the middle of a burning, glaring stretch of nothing-at-all. The desert was far off, as though it had been on another planet. The feeling of isolation and aloneness grew in him until everything became unreal, something from a nightmare that would leave him when he woke up.

But he knew that it was real enough; nothing could be so real as what had happened on this slope yesterday, and could easily happen again.

He felt his flesh chill as if a cold wind blew upon him. The glare and heat struck at him in a solid, harsh force, but at the same time he could feel that chill of knowing that the possibility of death was only seconds off.

All at once he seemed to see his body lying in the dust and glare of the slope, the little desert rodents snipping at his flesh. He felt a sudden awareness which filled him with the consciousness of life. He wanted to turn and run. He was living, he breathed and talked and thought and ate and slept. The pulses of desires and hopes, vague, unrealized plans, began to surge and pound—all the things he wished to do that he would never be able to do. For a space, the drive to run became so powerful in him that he had to take his gun in both hands to keep from dropping it at his feet.

He stopped, feeling the shaking in his limbs and body, trying to steady himself and steady the revolver in his hands. That was when he saw the

Indian. He came up in the slot between the slabs of rock beneath the trees, and lifted his bow. Patterson made him out in the instant that he appeared, and as he looked at him it seemed that all of his life was centered on that tiny focal point of bronze flesh and poised oblivion. All the years that he had lived on earth had shaped themselves, it seemed, as in some kind of pyramid, the apex resting in that cleft between the stone slabs.

He stood as firmly as he could. The blade of his revolver sight was on the slot and he could see the sunlight on the arch of the bow. Through the groove in the receiver, he could see the small, dark face, and then the hammer bulged above it into the line of sight. It surprised him, for he had no memory of releasing it; but now the sound was there, dull and wide against the hill, and then the arrow through the rag of smoke. And that surprised him, too, because it passed above him in a thin sigh that left him unhit and standing.

Then a second had skipped over in time, and he was now running. He was running toward the slot. It seemed the only thing for him to do, and though he marveled that he had the strength to do it, he was running all the same, the small stones jarring at the soles of his boots. He felt a strange release, a crazy and wild elation that burned in him, and now burst out of him and made him run.

He heard a yell, and it was him yelling, yelling as he ran up.

"Yi!" he shouted, while the stones slammed at his feet. "Yi!" he yelled again, and he could see the trees were very near now. Then he yelled again and fired at the same time, putting the barrel on the slot and seeing the rock chip off in a spray of dust when the bullet hit.

"Yi!" he yelled, and fired again at the slot above him.

He made himself go running and yelling all the way up there, until the rocks were right in front of him. He wasn't aware of reaching them, nor of the trees that arched their shadows over him, nor of going through the thin slot. He wasn't aware of much of anything now at all except the crazy wildness that had filled him, and of the shouting that kept coming up out of him, until the tank had, of a sudden, come to be before him. Had it not been for that, he might easily have gone on that way until he fell, or had been struck down.

But the tank was there, and now he had to catch himself from falling into it. He teetered on the edge, and in the moment of gaining his balance back, the yelling died out in him and he could feel his head begin to grow clear.

Then his head was quite clear, and he looked down. He saw it all at once, the way you see a thing before you fully understand what it is, or what it might mean. It might have been like a piece of china that had broken, and must be studied before the fragments can be glued and put together again. But a little at a time, the pieces fell back in place.

Wagner had been right about the number of Indians. There were three of them, although Patterson, at first, did not see the third one. He saw first the one who lay beneath the slot, where he had fallen when hit. He would be the one whose arrow had gone over him, and now he lay there with his head cracked, and a part of it laid open. Another one lay below, along the edge of the water, with the side of his neck torn wide in a ragged, very bloody wound. This one lay as if about to drink, but had been killed first, or had been hit and then had bled to death while trying to get water. There seemed to be a stiffness to his body and limbs, too, and Patterson had to search his mind before he thought of all the ricochets that must have slammed around inside these rock walls when he and Jager had been firing toward the slot in order to cover Muller. It seemed a long time back now, though it was just yesterday.

The third one could have killed him while he stood there gaping at the two dead ones; but he was trying to get away. He was scrambling up the far side of the tank, and when the move caught Patterson's eye it came to him that, once the shooting had started, the Indian had been more fearful than he was.

In a way, then, he felt sorry for him; and except that they would need the horses themselves in order to reach the settlements, he might have let him escape.

Still, he didn't have to shoot him in the back. For as he came out over the edge of the tank and came to his feet among the stone blocks, the Indian pulled a knife from his clout. And as he turned to throw it, all in one smooth motion of his rippling bronze body, Patterson raised his arm and fired into his chest.

After he had done that, there was a time when he had only the strength to find a broad stone and lie upon it and keep himself on it. He could feel his body shaking with the cost of running up the hill, and perhaps with fright, too. His lungs were puffing at the air and he could feel his heart slam back and forth in his chest.

He was lying in the shade, and he could feel the branches of the mesquite trees above shield him from the sunlight; and down below him in the water, he could see their interlaced reflections in the blue of the sky. Over beyond the trees a ways, an Indian pony nickered, as if asking what had happened.

All he wanted to do for now was lie in the shade for a while and pull himself together. In time he would be able to make his way down over the edge of the tank to the water; but he could not do that just yet. He had only strength enough to look at it for now, and to think how it would feel against his face and on his tongue and running down his dry throat.

Only slowly did he begin to understand that he would not be able to do it, even at that time. Another one of his stupid obligations had just come into his mind. For a moment it made him hate the Army with a hatred that, as it was so strong, he nearly could taste it. But in another moment, after it had grown and rounded in his mind, the feeling changed to something like pride.

It was now implied that he was an old campaigner, a veteran. Anyone who knew the Army knew, too, that no commander worth his salt would ever meet his own needs ahead of those of his troops. And down below him on the grim desert, Patterson's Irregulars, his first command, was waiting to be brought in to water.

God give him what it took to make it down there, and back here with them again.

John Prescott is the author of a small number of impressive Western novels and stories, all of them published during the 1950s and early 1960s. He was born in Menominee, Michigan, and educated at Lawrence College in Appleton, Wisconsin. During the Second World War he served in U.S. Army Air Force Heavy Bombardment Group. Following his discharge, he worked in the advertising agency business, writing fiction in his spare time. In 1951, he moved with his family to Phoenix, Arizona. His earliest books were written for children, prior to the appearance of his first Western, *The Renegade* (Random House, 1954). His second Western novel, *Journey by the River* (Random House, 1954), published in paperback as *Wagon Train*, won the Spur Award from the Western Writers of America in the category of best historical novel the same year it was published. His Western stories are distinguished by strong character development. His style, including "very realistic descriptions of the land and exceptionally good treatment of natural features and the weather," was praised by P.R. Meldrum for his entry on the author in *Twentieth Century Western Writers* (St. James Press, 1991). Among Prescott's notable later novels are *Ordeal* (Random House, 1958), *Valley of Wrath* (Fawcett Gold Medal, 1961), and *Treasure of the Black Hills* (Dell, 1962).

Center Point Large Print
600 Brooks Road / PO Box 1
Thorndike, ME 04986-0001 USA

(207) 568-3717

US & Canada:
1 800 929-9108
www.centerpointlargeprint.com